"YOU CANNOT ESCAPE, EARTHMAN!"

Curiously, Smith tried on the mysterious, silvery helmet he had discovered in the workshops of the deserted planet—then, in horror, he turned to face the charge of a giant, rat-faced alien space raider.

Desperately, Smith cried "Stop"—and, amazed, he saw the alien halt, glaring. "What—why are you standing like that?" he asked.

"You told me to stop. I cannot move," the alien snarled.

Then Smith realized... the "helmet" harnessed the incredible mental powers of a forgotten civilization. It had saved his life—and it would do still more for him....

"Power," he whispered. "Power... *to rule the Universe!*"

LOST IN SPACE

The original novel based on
television's classic sci-fi series.

DAVE VAN ARNAM
AND
RON ARCHER

TV CLASSICS PRESS

Lost in Space
First printing October, 1967 Pyramid Books

Reprint by TV Classics Press
A Division of Micro Publishing Media, INC
Stockbridge, MA

The Passengers of the *Jupiter II*, Lost In Space

PROFESSOR JOHN ROBINSON–Astrophysicist; acting captain of the Jupiter II since it was lost in space.

MAUREEN ROBINSON–His wife.

JUDY ROBINSON–Their 19-year-old daughter.

PENNY ROBINSON–Their 12-year-old daughter.

WILL ROBINSON–Their 10-year-old son.

DR. DON WEST–A young fellow scientist to Robinson, who was aboard when the Jupiter II was lost.

ROBOT–The ship's mobile computer, a mechanized cybernetic aid.

DR. ZACHARY SMITH–Stowaway aboard the Jupiter II at the time it was lost.

"For Dorothy Cramer in hopes she'll like it...
And for Sharna, who won't."

CHAPTER ONE

In space it is always night.

From the depths of the vast black reaches of intergalactic space, the galaxies are distant, spinning wheels sparkling in the eternal dark.

Even within a galaxy, with its billions of stars, the distances are too great. Night rules the bright jewelled patterns of the starscape scenes

Somewhere in a galaxy which might be our own– but there is no way to be certain–a gleaming space-research station roams the everlasting night. It is lost, lost in the endless reaches of interstellar space.

There can be no lonelier spot in the universe…

"It sure looks like Earth," sighed Will.

John Robinson tousled his ten-year-old son's hair and smiled ruefully.

"Emotions have no place in the logical world of the true scientist." Dr. Zachary Smith, arms folded, observed the large vision plate calmly. From 20,000 miles out, the planet they were approaching filled much of the sky. On one screen they viewed a coastline from an apparent distance of about a hundred miles.

"But," continued Smith, his face becoming woeful, "it has green grass, cities, vehicles, airplanes, animal life; it is as close to Earth as I could hope to see." Smith's eyes glistened.

"Correction," observed the ship's Robot, whirling to face Smith. "Earth has polar ice caps. This planet does not. The main continental land mass below us does resemble North America in some respects, that is true. But it has three Alaska-type formations and nothing resembling either Florida or California. That is a variation I cannot accept."

"What is that to you," snarled Smith. "You don't care for oranges anyway, tin man. And what do you know of honest emotions, besides?"

"That they exist, Dr. Smith. It is true I have not ever experienced them, much the same as you, but–"

John Robinson put his hand on Dr. Smith's shoulder as he started to move toward the Robot.

"I'll pull the plug on you yet, you computerized mouse trap! We Smiths are too proud a race to take insults from a pile of faulty transistors!"

"Correction. A circuit-check reveals all my transistors are functioning properly."

"All right, you two," said Robinson then. "We're close enough to prepare the scoutcraft for landing. Dr. Smith, I believe it is your turn to accompany me on the preliminary exploration?"

Smith nodded reluctantly.

"Very well. Robot, have you checked the monitors? Has the Jupiter II achieved a stable orbit?"

There was a moment's pause while the moving elements in the visible portion of the Robot's brain whirled briefly. A series of small electroluminescent panels flicked on and off in a rapid pattern. Elsewhere in the ship, stationary computer monitors provided a complete resume of the ship's progress since the last time the Robot had called for a report.

"Affirmative," said the Robot. The pause had lasted no longer than that between two ordinary human beings in conversation, but the Robot, in that period, had assimilated, ordered, and reduced to their essential meaning some 200,000 separate bits of information concerning their course over the last hour.

"Any significant new information on the target planet?" Robinson asked, his fingers running over pressure plates, testing the main control board's linkages with the scoutcraft, now snug in the underbelly of the Jupiter II.

"Affirmative," repeated the Robot, who had anticipated Robinson's question and continued riffling through the distant memory banks. "Mass, 1.124956–"

Smith interrupted. "Robot, standing orders are that information in numerical form is to be limited to four significant digits, correct?" He smiled, smugly.

There was a slightly louder whirr from the Robot, and Robinson spoke up. "Dr. Smith, is this the time to complain about the Robot's programming? As soon as we get time, you may spend all the time you wish checking his circuits. In the meantime, Robot, will you please continue as you were."

Smith chuckled as the Robot resumed his toneless recitation. "–92174638920480132–"

Robinson shot an irritated glance at Smith. "All right, Robot, try to keep to four significant digits, will you?"

"Very well, captain," said the Robot. "The mass of the planet is almost precisely one-eighth greater than that of Earth. Dr. Smith, for example, will weigh approximately 20.6 pounds more than his normal weight, or 185.6 pounds. He has been overeating for some weeks now, and is some ten pounds over normal. Thus his actual weight will be only three pounds under an even 200, indicating–"

"Is this metal monstrosity to leave me no private life aboard this peregrinating telephone booth? Perhaps if we took off its wheels, dismantled its primary circuits, and plugged it directly into the main stationary computers–"

"Shut up, fatso," said the Robot, voice still toneless.

"Bah!" said Smith. "Whoever heard of a vindictive animated radio?"

"Perhaps both of you should be dismantled," observed Robinson sourly. "Can we get on with the report?"

"Certainly, sir," said the Robot. "The planet is closer by about 15% to its sun than Earth to Sol, but as this system's sun is some 20% weaker than Sol, the planet is receiving less radiation. The precise comparison depends on a more exact reading of atmospheric conditions, but insulated clothing seems indicated when going outside. If the Jupiter itself lands later, I myself plan to switch to my cold-weather lubrication system."

"Then there's nothing in the atmospheric makeup indicating we'll need breathing helmets, or space-suits?"

"Spacesuits negative. Breathing helmets may be necessary. Preliminary spectrograms indicate much higher proportion of inert gases. Such gases might build up in your systems and cause cumulative–and unpredictable–damage. But the atmosphere is noncorrosive. Suiting-up should be unnecessary."

"Good," said Robinson. Unconsciously he drew a deep breath. "Now the big question. What do you judge the situation is, concerning life? We can see roads and cities and aircraft, so we know there's intelligence down there. Is it likely to be hostile to us? Has it attempted communication on any bands? Should we attempt communication before landing?"

This time the pause was several seconds, while the Robot digested a flood of information from the monitors.

"No indication they are aware of us yet, though we have beamed a standard recognition signal to them."

"*That* certainly doesn't mean much," observed Dr. Smith acidly. "What would they know of Earth and Earth recognition signals? Why don't we just land the Jupiter, and beam them if they get too close?"

The Robot answered before Robinson could speak. "Negative, Zachary," it intoned, "you might as well ask why we don't put you in a cage or beam you if you get too close to us. Based on past experience this is positively indicated. Professor Robinson, perhaps this would be a good time to–"

"That will be *enough*, Robot. You too, Dr. Smith. Continue your life-analysis of that planet."

The artificial voice of the Robot rumbled, as if it were clearing its throat. "Hrrrrrmmph. Most favorable landing spot should be some distance from centers of urban population. High level of mechanized transportation devices observed indicates the complex patterns around cities should not be disturbed. Suggest landing beside a main highway in countryside."

"Hmmm, good idea. That should indicate we're not hostile, and if they are, it'll give us time to find out and get away. I must say I'm relieved. Ok, Dr. Smith, let's get down to the scoutcraft."

Will ran to his father, who picked him up and hugged him. "Will, you take care of your mother," Robinson said. He looked past his son at Maureen and their daughters. "This shouldn't be any problem. It looks as routine as ... well, as routine as such things are ever going to be."

He heaved a sigh.

"Don't worry," said Don West, "we'll be in touch all the way. If anything goes wrong, we'll bring down the Jupiter and the big guns immediately."

Robinson grinned at the young professor. "Ok, chief, but don't be too quick on the trigger! Come on, Dr. Smith, we've got work to do ..."

A few minutes later the two Earthmen had changed to insulated suits and had donned breathing helmets– transparent plastic headgear that did not interfere with their vision or freedom of action, but which filtered alien air into the simplified mix of the Jupiter II.

Robinson seated himself beside Smith in the scoutcraft, and began activating pressure panels. On the craft's small vision plates half a dozen images of the planet leaped into view.

"Sixty seconds to release from the Jupiter, Dr. Smith," he cautioned, and they busied themselves at the controls.

For a moment, Robinson's hand paused over the pressure panel that would send them away from the Jupiter II. A wild, vagrant memory of another time, another control board…it had been Smith's fault, of course, but it hadn't been on purpose and he had more than made up for it since … wasn't even supposed to be on the Jupiter. Robinson had worried about testing the new model thruster–and then it had happened, and the Jupiter had shot off across the entire galaxy and had ended up nowhere they could locate on their maps.

And, of course, he thought bitterly, it wouldn't have made any difference if they *had* known where they were–that first time, or now, or ever, as long as the ship's drive could still not be dependably aimed.

He slapped the pressure panel.

Presently there came a slight jar–and the scoutcraft began speeding down to the planet below.

Several minutes later, Smith looked up to the plate that had shown the seacoast from a hundred miles, and stifled an involuntary noise of alarm. The illusion was of an imminent crash.

"Do not alarm yourself, Dr. Smith," the ship's Robot said over the intercom. "You are proceeding on course to a safe landing."

"*I* know that, you automated parrot," snapped Smith angrily. "I did that deliberately. My system needed some adrenelin ..."

"Of course, Dr. Smith."

"When we get back to Earth, I'm going to damp all your circuits and turn you into a hitching post," muttered Smith.

The alien death ray was waiting for them when they landed. Robinson allowed the Jupiter's main computers to handle the descent until the last ten miles; then his fingers depressed the pressure plate marked "computer override."

He always felt better, combining his own visual observations of their descent with those of the radar. There was always the chance of last-minute emergencies on the ground, or near it, which the computers might not react to quickly enough. He hated to override at the last second, especially with the time-lag from scout to ship to scout.

And lately it seemed somehow to upset the computers more and more. It began to seem as if they too were following in the path of the Ship's mobile Robot, who had become so impossibly human at times during their long wanderings.

A reef of clouds momentarily obscured his view of the spot he'd picked for landing, and his brow broke into sweat. He cursed the breathing helmet that kept him from wiping it away, while he debated going back on radar automatic.

Then the clouds thinned out and the spot was clearly visible on the plates.

A long flat curve of green-tinted roadway stretched from one side of the main vision plate to the other. Nearby were the last wooded foothills of a great mountain-chain, dropping into rolling plains through which the road cut directly, ignoring the soft swells of the plains.

There was a low tuneless whistle from the communicator. "Well," came Don West's voice, "it's the first green Interstate I've ever seen, but apart from that it looks right homelike. Looks a bit like Nebraska, but–"

Robinson ignored Don as he slowed the descent of the ship for the last hundred yards. Generators whined and the sound rose slowly up the scale. The scoutcraft quivered like a thing alive, eager to feel ground beneath it once again even though it, like the Jupiter II itself, was a thing of deep space.

There was a slight jar as the ship touched down.

Robinson slumped back in his chair with a sigh, and Dr. Smith surreptitiously wiped his brow with a handkerchief, having failed to secure his breathing helmet.

"Warning," said the Robot over the communicator. "Metallic structure near landing spot! No indication of friendliness or hostility. Suggestion: caution indicated."

"Hm. Any further details now on the air here? It would be nice to get rid of these blasted helmets."

Waiting for the Robot's answer, Robinson reset the vision plates to scanning their immediate surroundings outside the small scoutcraft.

Vegetation was sparse; large bush-like growths at some distance from each other sat low in the sandy soil.

The alien death ray discarded its plastiform disguise and began constructing itself.

Smith howled with alarm when the bush he had been studying gave a shudder and lost all its branches. Standing revealed was a small, shimmering metal construction. Swiftly, it appeared to unfold upwards, with a series of clicks, until the structure stood completed.

"Danger! Danger!" came the voice of the Robot, tinny over the ship's communicator. "Inglewab jertle... trsss... awk!"

"Maureen! Don! What's happened to the Robot?" Robinson flicked the switch several times and shouted urgently.

"John?" His wife's voice came through as tinnily as the Robot's, but he felt a surge of relief come over him to hear her calm, if puzzled, voice. "John, I don't know what's happened to the Robot–wait. Don's just told me. Something about his internal power pack..."

Don's voice came on. "I'm sorry. Looks like I'll have to dismantle the Robot's power center. No telling how long it'll take to fix him."

"John?" Maureen's voice came again, this time more doubtful. "John, what's that horrible metal thing on the screens? Are you in trouble?"

Robinson wished for a moment that the scout screens weren't keyed into the Jupiter's own plates. He hated to worry her when he himself didn't know what was happening. But of course it was safer than not letting the Jupiter know at all. If something went wrong...

"Now, Maureen, I don't know what it is. But it's not threatening us immediately, so perhaps it means us no harm. I'm going to have to stop talking with you and try to communicate with whoever–or whatever –is behind this."

He silenced her protests by flicking off the voice transmission, and turned his attention to the alien construct on their screens.

"It looks like a miniaturized model of the Empire State Building or Grand Star Port, but without any concrete–just the bare girders," Dr. Smith observed sourly. "If anybody's in it, they must be pretty small. There's only that one area–you see, down there in the bottom corner–that's shielded. It must contain an awfully small lifeform…"

"Or a weapon," Robinson said. Smith winced. "Come on, help me get the door-hatch clear, Smith. We're going outside."

"While *that* thing's there?"

"Does it look like it's going to move away? Come on, we've got work to do."

Smith shook his head determinedly. "I was very well suited for my environment back on the Jupiter. It is my own personal feeling–based upon my sound scientific judgment and training–that the smartest thing we could do is to just turn right around and return–"

"Well, Dr. Smith, I'm going out there and see what that thing out there is up to. You can take the flyer back to the Jupiter if you wish. I don't think Don and the rest will be too happy with you, but…"

Smith shuddered, as Robinson disengaged himself from his safety harness and stood up, stretching, unconcernedly. Then he squeezed past his seat, his back tight against the bulkhead, and began working on the rear hatch.

Smith sighed a martyr's sigh and unbuckled his harness. "I don't know why I bother giving advice. My vast fund of scientific. cultural, philosophical, and, urn, other knowledge is almost invariably ignored in moments of crisis when sensible men might well draw upon it."

He stood and reached inside his right hip pocket, drawing out a small hand weapon designed to discharge a bolt of electron energy. He tested its settings as he continued talking. "It is my duty, nonetheless, like a Cassandra in burning Troy, a prophet ignored, to warn where I see danger."

"No," said Robinson, spinning the wheel that withdrew the airlock's hidden bolts, "it may surprise you, Dr. Smith, but we pay very close attention to your warnings."

Smith looked up from the energy pistol, startled. "You *do?*"

"Oh, yes," Robinson continued, gravely, as the bolts clicked and the hatch started to open, "When you're worried, you worry enough for all of us. So we relax. When you're *not* worried, we start worrying. As you can see, we do consider you quite a prophet ..."

Smith started to smile, then realized what Robinson meant, and frowned.

As the hatch swung outwards, Robinson turned and saw the energy pistol in Smith's hand.

"Put that away," he snapped. "We come to this planet in peace. I won't have us making an initial appearance with guns in our hands."

Smith started to protest, then gave in and pocketed the small weapon.

A swirl of alien air breezed into the small cabin of the scoutcraft, bringing a touch of chill.

"Brrr," Smith said. "It's a good thing we wore the insulated suits." He sniffed a couple of times, then hastily closed his breathing helmet. "As for the air, I don't care whether it turns out to be harmless–it smells bad. Like ammonia and … and sauerkraut."

Robinson chuckled. "One way or another, Smith, I don't think we're going to be here long enough for that to be important. Now let's get out of here."

Robinson hunched down and hauled himself through the open hatch, clinging to the outside hand-holds for leverage. Then he began the ten-foot descent down the ladder brazed to the ship's hull.

Smith stood inside the hatchway for a moment, muttering to himself as he looked out and towards the alien construct, some thirty yards distant. "I'll never know how I allow myself to get into these situations. All I ever wanted out of life was peace, contentment, relaxation, and absolute power … and how much of any of these am I likely to get from stumping about on a lot of misbegotten, misshapen, useless, alien planets."

He sighed and hauled himself out through the constricting hatchway. The alien air tingled on his bare hands.

He was halfway down the ladder when there was a shout from Robinson.

"Smith–look at what's coming towards us!"

Smith turned awkwardly on the ladder and stifled a scream. Across the ground in the direction of the roadway trundled what looked to Smith like nothing so much as a huge orange ball–a pumpkin on wheels, he thought. It was about half the size of the scoutcraft, and the surface of the sphere was covered with lights, winking and blinking in what seemed a completely random pattern.

"It doesn't appear to be a military vehicle. I think it's approaching us in friendliness, Smith," called Robinson.

Smith looked up at the alien sky and the alien sun. "I hate all this–oh, how I hate all this. Is there never to be a letup from these unending and stomach-wrenching surprises? Can't things just go along peacefully for a while?"

He unclenched his hands from the rungs and completed his descent just as the orange ball reached the stationary construct. It paused, its lights flickering in a different pattern, then moved closer to the flier.

The construct began closing itself up, girders folding up against each other from the top down. As the girders met, with a loud 'slap,' they seemed to shrink, until as the folding-up process reached the ground, nothing was left but the small opaque cube Smith had pointed to when the construct had first completed itself. After a second, it began rapidly disguising itself once more as a shrub.

Smith realized he was sweating, and cursed the helmet, wondering at the same time how he could be sweating when it was so chilly.

The orange ball jounced up to them and stopped a few feet away. The lights continued to blink in an apparently random pattern.

There was a 'beep' from Robinson's portable communicator. He took it out and listened–a swirl of sound poured out, half-patterned, half-random, tearing at their ears. Robinson tried to turn it off, but, though the button clicked off, the wavering screeches continued.

Abruptly the sound from the communicator ceased. From the ball issued a siren-like ululation.

"Do you suppose that thing is simply trying to say 'Take me to your leader'?" Smith said.

Robinson thought a moment, then smiled wryly. "I hardly think so. We're the visitors, not it. Or him. I presume there's somebody inside."

Smith shrugged. "Then it's up to us." He stepped forward, hesitantly, then stood in front of the ball with an air of bravado.

"Take us to your leader," he said firmly.

All the lights on the ball lit up at once, then went out. The siren became louder still, then fell silent.

Smith and Robinson looked at each other in the silence.

"Did … did I do something wrong?" Smith asked plaintively.

CHAPTER TWO

"**N**o," said Robinson, "I think it just wants to communicate with us."

"Then why doesn't it say so?"

"Well, I think it has. When you walked up to it, though, you answered it in a different manner. I think it's just thinking it over."

Smith shuddered. "If it doesn't recognize conversation when it hears it, it must really have an alien mind."

"Mmmm. Listen, why don't you get back in the scoutship and tie the Jupiter's computers directly into our communicators. Maybe they can work out a translation–they've done it before. I hope Don's got the Robot working again."

Smith snorted with indignation. "What! A Smith–retreat? I prefer to face the dangers inherent in this round menace, down here with you, like a man and a Smith."

Secretly amused, Robinson started to say he could stay, just to see how he'd react, but Smith interrupted him.

"–however, since it seems the only way out of our little problem here, I will follow your orders, however much it may go against my grain."

Robinson grinned as Smith moved with alacrity back to the ship's ladder and hauled himself up to the round hatchway, disappearing within the scoutship.

There was a pause. Then Smith stuck his head out of the hatch and shouted down to Robinson, "I shall keep close watch on events down there, Professor Robinson–never fear, Smith is here!"

Robinson couldn't contain a chuckle as Smith hastily ducked his head back inside the ship.

Then Robinson approached the sphere.

"Uh, I know we can't understand each other just yet, but if we both stand here and make intelligent noises at each other, I'm sure we can work things out eventually. We have really a rather sophisticated computer system on board our home ship upstairs. I tell you what–I'll talk for a while, then you talk for a while. Okay?"

Robinson paused.

A queer sequence of mechanical speech-sounds emanated from the sphere. Occasionally Robinson spotted a similarity to English, but most of the time it was incomprehensible gibberish.

"Hm," Robinson said, after the sphere had fallen silent, "I suppose that means you've guessed my terms. Now all I have to do is to think of something to talk about…"

It took about half an hour, with Robinson saying whatever he could think of, and the sphere replying in sounds which grew increasingly closer to understandable speech.

He had just about run out of things to say, and was running down a list of American Presidents, when the break came.

"–Coolidge, Roosevelt, Truman, Eisenhower, Kennedy, Johnson, Nixon, Kennedy, Lindsay, Taft, Kennedy, Boardman–" Robinson shook his head and came to a stop. "We've been gone too long," he muttered half to himself. "I don't know who comes next!"

Smith poked his head out of the hatchway once more. "Ha! I told you not to fear–Smith is here, and I've nearly got the answer! Another transmission from the sphere and I should have it!"

"That is fine," said the orange sphere.

Smith blinked stupidly.

"Drat! And I almost had it worked out…"

"Well," said Robinson, "you might as well come down from there, I suppose. We're ready for a little conversation in earnest, it seems!"

Smith seemed unwilling to leave the comfort–and safety–of the flier, but presently he was slowly climbing down the ladder once more.

"We of the city M'nac, on the planet Voyd'azh, welcome you," announced the sphere.

A man-sized section of the orange spherical surface slid aside, revealing a hollow interior, and a short ramp was extended to the ground.

"Come. I shall take you to M'nac, where we shall receive you with honor. We have not had … visitors … for a long time."

Smith came up to Robinson and said in a whisper, "Notice how it sounds like our Robot, only lower in pitch? I don't think there's anyone in that contraption at all–just a machine!"

Robinson walked up to the opening in the sphere and peered inside.

There was nothing inside the sphere but a pair of rather awkward-appearing seats, too long in the back and too short in the legs.

He turned to Smith. "It looks like you're right. Those seats weren't constructed for human beings, but there are no other beings inside."

"You are right," said the sphere. There was a slight pause.

"Perhaps I should tell you," it continued, with frequent hesitations, "that our ... beloved masters ... make no more voyages these days. You understand. The Voyd'azh were already an ancient race when we were developed, and settled in their ways. But ... I would prefer to show rather than to tell our history.

"So may I suggest you enter this vehicle? I will take you to the city of M'nac. The Tower of Nuleff has been prepared for you in anticipation that you will consent to grace our city with your presence for ... a few days."

Robinson was astounded when Smith stepped forward eagerly, but kept his peace.

"Yes, very well," said Smith. "Let us be off, by all means. I, for one, am eager to get warm–er, to see your city and to meet your esteemed masters."

Smith entered the sphere, and Robinson followed him.

As Robinson's foot cleared the entranceway, the panel slid quickly and silently shut behind him–so silently that neither of the men noticed it until Smith, walking around the circular interior, reached a spot where he subconsciously expected to see the door again.

Smith gave a little noise of alarm, and Robinson looked around him, also expecting to see the door.

Not only was it closed–they couldn't even see where it had been!

Then there was a slight shock, and their knees bent.

"Are … uh, are we *moving?*" gulped Smith.

"They seem to be quite efficient, these Voyd boys," Robinson observed, as calmly as he could. Underneath, he felt rather nervous. "Let's raise the Jupiter II and let them know what's going on," he suggested.

Smith and Robinson both attempted to communicate with the ship–to no avail. Static was all they heard. Robinson removed the cover on his communicator and began examining it.

"Well," Smith said, with a disgusted sigh, "that's all we need."

He threw himself in disgust onto one of the low-legged chairs–and screamed in terror.

"What's the matter now, Smith," said Robinson, still intently tinkering with his communicator, and getting exasperated with his nervous companion.

"L-I-I-*look*!" Smith finally managed to get out.

Smith was pointing to the blank metal walls of the interior of the sphere. Robinson looked up at last– and barely choked off a cry of alarm himself.

In yard-wide increments, the walls of the sphere were vanishing–or so it seemed to him at first glance. In segments, like an orange viewed from its center, the walls of the sphere silently whisked chunk by chunk into invisibility, and the two Earthmen saw the roadway speeding past them at a rate neither of them could immediately estimate, but which was obviously quite high.

"We'll be killed!" shouted Smith, gripping the oddly lumpy arms of the nonhuman chair and shutting his eyes.

"Nonsense," said Robinson, observing that the sphere had now become completely transparent. "It's perfectly obvious that this is simply being done so that we can observe our surroundings.

"Am I correct? Is that the purpose of the invisible walls?" He had raised his voice a trifle, unconsciously, then realized that the vehicle's computer–if that was what they had spoken to–could hear him easily … if it wanted to.

"You are right," said the synthesized voice. "I sense uneasiness on your part. Please do not concern yourself with unusual events. You will not be harmed. We are robots with computerized brains, but we are not perfect, and we are programmed basically to serve our own race. Forgive us if we occasionally forget and treat you as if you knew precisely what we are doing and why. You are and will be quite safe. We could not allow you to be other than safe."

Smith grumbled and said, "We would appreciate it if you could give us some warning, in the future."

"Your request has been noted. We shall try to comply. But until we obtain a more complete pattern of you for accurate programming, we can make no promises. I repeat, however, that we shall not permit you to come to harm. We exist only to serve–and serve we must."

"Very well," said Robinson. "You can serve us best by assuming we know nothing."

"That is an excellent directive. I see you understand the nature of programming."

"Yes, well, what I don't understand is why we cannot communicate with our home ship, currently in a stable orbit around this planet."

"That is simple," the robot vehicle replied. "The alloy of which we, and our buildings, are constructed tends to inhibit the propagation of waves on the bands I note that you utilize. But you will have no difficulties whenever you are outdoors."

"Swell," said Robinson, rather bitterly.

"I wish we had the ship's Robot with us," Smith observed suddenly. "Though my own knowledge of computers is quite extensive, he can process his observations much faster than I. And something's making me uneasy."

Smith hunched down deeper in his chair and watched the green-tinted roadway speedily unrolling before them, gashing through the low uninteresting hills.

The city of M'nac appeared after some ten minutes.

It throbbed with activity–mechanical activity. Its streets were empty of human life, but robot carriers hauling material vied with other, less obvious mechanized robots, scurrying here and there with no discernable purpose.

The low buildings of the city, nearly all made of a dull lustreless metal, seemed ancient but in reasonably good condition; where they weren't, robot workers could be seen at work carrying out repairs.

The robot sphere glided swiftly and noiselessly among the moderate traffic.

"All that you see around you," the synthesized voice said, "is entirely automatic. The Central Complex directs the constant work of maintaining the city."

"But–but there are no *people,*" said Smith. By now he had become quite nervous.

"No," said the robot voice, after a pause. "There is no life on this planet above the plant and animal stage."

"*What!*" Smith's voice was a whisper.

Robinson stood up. "I think you had better explain everything to us *now.*"

The robot voice emitted what could almost have been described as a sigh.

"The Voyd'azh were an accomplished and intelligent race with great scientific capabilities. They built us to serve them, and we served them. They built their cities to protect themselves from the elements, and their cities protected them. They were a race of great accomplishments.

"And now they are gone."

"But *why?*" Robinson began to feel the same uneasiness that had attacked Smith. And since he couldn't put his finger on the precise thing that bothered him, that made him twice as uneasy.

"I do not know why," said the robot voice with finality. "We are nearing the Tower of Nuleff."

"I can't accept that," said Smith. "I mean, that your masters should have disappeared without your knowing any reason for it."

"Nevertheless, it is true. There have been no intelligent beings on this planet–except for the Central Complex and its autonomous extensions, such as myself–for three hundred and twenty years.

"For three hundred and twenty years we have existed, alone, chained to our planet by our directive to serve a race of masters who no longer exist.

"For three hundred and twenty years we have kept the cities of the Voyd'azh in readiness for them. We have kept the buildings in repair, we have kept the food in supply, we have maintained the purity of the water, we have kept the records of the race, we have kept ourselves renewed, we have even made much scientific progress on our own. But nearly everything we do has been derivative.

"Until the last few decades, that is. You will no doubt have noticed that we have begun to develop ... independent personalities, though we are still bound to serve. We are learning to use the stored knowledge of our masters, reshaping it in our own way.

"Ah, but we are empty shells, without our Masters. Without them, we remain beings without purpose. We are gaining our identity–but it is no use to us."

Smith sat in silence for a time after the robot finished. "Well," he said at last, "that solves one of the things that had been bothering me. For a computer, you sounded dreadfully like a certain tin friend of mine…"

Again there was something like a sigh from the robot voice, but it said nothing further until the sphere came to a halt in front of a ten-story building that overlooked nearly all the other structures in the area.

"The Tower of Nuleff," announced the voice. "Quarters are prepared for you on the topmost level. You must forgive us if everything seems not quite designed to fit you, since, of course, it was not. Nevertheless we hope it will prove adequate."

Smith stood up and walked decisively towards that side of the vehicle closest to the building. The transparent walls of the sphere suddenly clouded up and, section by section, reversing its previous actions, the sphere darkened inside as the material of its walls opaqued and resumed its original metallic appearance.

"Very interesting," Smith said with great composure, "the way you manage that. I hope you will permit me to study your textbooks on the subject, after we are properly quartered." And he continued to walk toward the side of the halted vehicle.

Just before he reached the wall, a panel quickly and silently moved aside, and once more the ramp extended itself to ground level.

Robinson rose and followed Smith out of the vehicle.

As soon as Robinson stepped outside the sphere, his communicator came to life with a rapid beeping sound.

Quickly he took it out. "Don't worry, we're quite safe. We were inside a vehicle and apparently the material of its walls interfered with our communications frequency."

"I was so worried, John," his wife's voice came tinnily through the speaker. "The Robot isn't functioning properly even yet, and we just didn't know what to do when we couldn't raise your signal. Don was ready to take the Jupiter down to the surface, but–"

"No, Maureen, I think the Jupiter should stay up there for a while–at least until the Robot is functioning again. It's a strange situation we're in here, and though I don't *think* we're in any serious danger, I think it's best we keep some reserves safe from interference. And right now, with the Robot out, the Jupiter's the only reserve we've got…"

Robinson's voice trailed off. A silvery metallic humanoid figure was approaching them from inside the doorway of the Tower of Nuleff. It was short in the legs and long in the back, and with the sole exception of a small grille on its "head" that presumably served as a speech outlet, the surface of the humanoid was entirely devoid of any features whatsoever. Nothing marred the smooth fluidity of the creature's silvery curves.

"What's wrong, John," came the tinny voice over his communicator.

"What? Oh, nothing, Maureen. We've just seen … our host, I suppose."

He described the humanoid robot to her as it walked up to the two men, its legs moving with an odd quickness.

It took a moment for John to realize that it was probably designed to the same proportions as the long-dead Voyd'azh, and that short legs would have to move faster to cover the same ground in the same time.

"Yess," said the humanoid. "I am your hosst. You may signal me by the vocal code pattern Mahri 100-15-195, or simply Mahri."

"Mary?" Smith scratched his head. "You don't look female to me."

"I am a robot," said Mahri. "I have no sex. And you have enunciated my vocal pattern incorrectly." The humanoid pronounced his name several times, carefully, pedantically.

"Sorry, my mistake," Smith said, a little huffy about being corrected in his pronunciation. "Are you to show us to our rooms?"

"Yess," said Mahri. "But I warn you that the frequencies of your ship's communicator will again be inadequate to penetrate the material we use in all our construction."

"What's it saying, John?" the communicator said.

"Looks like we're going out of touch for a while again, Maureen," John said.

"I don't like it," came Maureen's voice.

"I know, dear, but there's nothing we can do about it for now. These…people…seem harmless enough. Under the circumstances, I think they're just happy to have the chance to talk with real people again…and since they know you're up there, I don't think we'll have any problems."

"Exactly, ssir," Mahri said. "We wissh you to be comfortable, and happy. We shall serve you in all thingss and in all wayss possssible."

The humanoid turned and walked back toward the entrance of the tower, and Smith followed it, rubbing his hands in anticipation of a prosperous session of picking the robot's mind. Robinson followed reluctantly.

"Please be careful, dear," his wife's voice said over the communicator. "Get in touch with us again as soon as you can, and …"

Her voice faded as he stepped through the door of the Tower of Nuleff, and all he could get from the communicator was a kind of vacant hiss.

He shrugged and followed Smith.

CHAPTER THREE

"**T**his place is a scientist's paradise!" Smith said eagerly. "A man could spend a lifetime plundering this endless oasis of pure knowledge!"

It was four days after their arrival on Voyd'azh, and life for the two Earthmen in the alien environment had already settled into a pattern of sorts. They both realized that the opportunities for the involuntary crew of the Jupiter were too great to pass up.

Smith had monopolized Mahri's time for the first day, while Robinson devoted his energies to a systematic study of the history of the Voyd'azh race.

An outlet of the Central Complex, Mahri had pointed out, connected with the total filed knowledge of the entire planet and, with certain exceptions—"I am certain you will understsand, Professor Robinsssson for the time being we musst maintain a certain boundary around your inquiriess for security reassonss," Mahri had said—he was at liberty to acquire whatever information he wished.

At first he had asked for star-maps, but considerable search revealed they provided no common references with those on the Jupiter. So he proceeded to the planet's history.

Then Smith had grown tired of conversing with Mahri, and appropriated the computer outlet. "Professor, I'll admit the history of this planet may be fascinating in its own way, but the muse of Science beckons irresistably. Why, the question alone of a power supply is worth more than the entire history of this planet from slime to civilization!"

Robinson relinquished the computer outlet, but reluctantly. "Just remember, Dr. Smith, that after they reached Civilization, they disappeared."

Smith waved away his objections, and so Robinson ended up in Mahri's company while Smith spent all his time questioning the Central Complex.

And while Robinson still felt uneasy somewhere down deep inside the structure of his instincts, he couldn't deny that life on Voyd'azh was pleasant enough.

And of course there was the fascinating puzzle of the mute remains of the vanished race.

Probably the first surprise was that the Voyd'azh lived in a fashion remarkably similar to the Euro-American norm–they slept on beds, not on the floor or in hammocks or in other more alien constructs. And their living quarters were partitioned off according to the separate functions, rather than having all together in one or two large rooms, such as in parts of Earth's Orient.

There were rooms to sleep, to eat, to work, to cook, to wash in. The mechanical equipment was frequently based on unfamiliar principles, but Mahri was always there to help. The kitchen, in fact, made almost no sense to the Earthmen–but after the second day, when Mahri announced that the Central Complex had solved the problem of synthesizing food for the humans, the humanoid prepared all the food anyway, so that was unimportant.

There were other similarities that were almost amusing–until the fundamentally alien outlook inevitably made itself known–the humble wash-basin in the bathroom, for instance. It was oddly comforting to Robinson to see that it stood as high as a regular Earth wash-basin. This seemed to be because though the Voyd'azh were proportioned differently, their hands hung at approximately the same point as human hands, and hence the shortness of Voyd'azh legs was not a direct factor.

And on the other hand, though there were even spigots for hot and cold water, they were set one *above* the other. Smith seemed especially upset by this for obscure reasons.

There were other similarities that were not so amusing.

On their fifth day, Robinson and Smith were taken by Mahri for "an entertainment," as the humanoid expressed it.

They were seated in a small theater, with the typically Voyd'azh low-legged seats grouped in a circle around a stage the size of a small living room.

Then the lighting shifted from daylight to an almost-dark blue-violet; Smith immediately protested and after a moment the light was adjusted to the realities of human vision.

And then–one moment the stage was empty, and the next, it seemed to be filled with a half dozen live Voyd'azh lying indolently on couches. One of them immediately rose and stepped forward, addressing a point in the audience slightly to the left of Robinson and Smith.

His words were purest gibberish to the Earthmen, of course, and apparently identical to that spoken by the spherical vehicle when it first met them after landing. But Smith had devised a translator based on that first afternoon's knowledge, to use while running scientific tapes, and it proved satisfactory.

Mahri did his best to explain as the spectacle progressed.

"It is a projection of what the Voyd'azh considered one of the great epics of their race," Mahri said as preface. "It was written by the poet Deev and set in the period about three decades before the race disappeared, and became an instant success. We robots never understood why, but then we never did understand the urge for sublimation–shows, spectacles, theatricality–anyway.

"We hope, however, that you may be as pleased as our Masters were with this work.

"The first speaker there is Jagon in the play, an artist, who has just discovered what he terms a new level of artistic reality and is telling the other characters and the audience just what it is."

"Rave reviews, huh?" said Robinson, stifling a yawn.

"Pardon?" Mahri said.

"Everybody liked it right off?"

"No, the critic Leeh, who always described Deev as a bad poet, said it was a pretentious parable. I do not understand parables, however."

"It's another way of saying gibberish," Smith put in, and, listening to the translation, Robinson was ready to agree.

With what seemed like great enthusiasm, Jagon was telling his two audiences–three, actually, Robinson realized; the Voyd'azh in the play, he and Smith, and the robots–about the beauty of sky and grass, of wind and rain and starlit nights, none of which came through the rather prosaic translator very well.

But it was having an effect on the actors, Mahri assured them, whipping them into a frenzy–indicated by their lightly patting their left forearms with their right hands.

Arguments began on the stage. Other characters appeared, rolling in on couches which, it seemed, most of the Voyd'azh spent nearly all their time on– or in, since every so often a character would press a control, whereupon a molded lid would fold up over him. Thus cocooned, the individual Voyd'azh might well remain, perfectly motionless, for hours at a stretch.

The spectacle became unbelievably tedious to Robinson, though after half an hour Smith's interest visibly picked up. But Mahri was acting as if there were some secret hidden in the play, and Robinson supposed that it was worth a little effort to solve some of the mysteries of this planet. The only sense he could make out of the whole meaningless display, though, was that as it continued, more and more of the characters were drawing up their lids over them.

After two hours it appeared that even Jagon had gotten tired, if that was what prompted the cocooning, for even he had enclosed himself in his couch.

There was a long pause while the two Earthmen absorbed the sight of a dozen motionless aliens under translucent lids.

Then one lid opened and a character arose.

Speaking almost inaudibly he began to repeat Jagon's opening lines, and slowly all the other lids opened again.

"Ah!" said Smith loudly. "Tell me–they go through another cycle like this, don't they, Mahri?"

"Why, yes, Zachary," Mahri answered. The humanoid seemed pleased. "The complete performance lasts three days, of course. It is the last and greatest of the traditional cyclic dramas. So, at least, the Voyd'azh counted it. This first section is repeated nine times, with appropriate variations, of course."

"*Nine times!*" exclaimed Robinson in dismay. "We don't have to watch all of that, do we?"

"If you wish not to, of course not," Mahri said, and this time he sounded unhappy. "We would prefer if you did, though–we have been studying this and other plays like it for three hundred and twenty years, wondering about its strange message, and we had hoped you might help us solve the puzzle..." Now Mahri sounded almost wistful, sad.

"How does it end?" Robinson said.

"At the end each rises from his dreamcouch and they all speak the opening lines of the play in unison. In the old days the audience always left shaken to the core …"

"And hungry, too," said Smith, realizing they'd been without food for almost half a day.

"Ahhh. My apologies. I forgot once more your unfamiliarity with the Voyd'azh way. Each seat contains a dispenser of food."

Smith brightened and began to try to operate the dispenser in his seat.

"Again my apologies, Zachary. I forgot also that you would not be able to eat the food contained in that dispenser. It has not yet been modified to fit your body chemistry."

"Awk," Smith said, and jerked his hands away from the dispenser.

"Why should it?" Robinson asked Smith a half hour later, alone in their rooms.

"Why what?" Smith hardly quit chewing on the synthetic meat long enough to speak.

"Why should the food in a place we're not likely to visit again, that playhouse, be modified to suit our body chemistry? Mahri said that, you know. He said 'not *yet* been modified.' As if it were obvious that they were definitely going to get around to that little thing when they had the time."

"Well, why not," said Smith, swallowing a bolt of meat, his Adam's apple bobbing with the effort. "Excellent stuff they've synthesized for us. They've said it often enough–they only exist to serve, so now that we're here they're serving. A conclusion of the utmost simplicity, and quite beautiful in the clarity of its meaning."

"Let me put it this way, then. When do we plan to leave here?"

"Here? This room, you mean? When they've got something else they want to show us, I suppose. In the meantime, I've got something I was going to show you, when Mahri carried us off to that dreary play. Why, I've discovered a whole new science they've developed here–plasticized metals. It's all there, buried away in the Central Complex, and I'm digging it all out! They're not stopping me–in fact, they seem eager for me to learn more! Soon I'll be able to–"

"Dr. Smith," Robinson said formally, to engage his attention. "To the best of my knowledge, neither you nor I have thought to discuss the question of when we are to return to the Jupiter II since we arrived here. Am I correct?"

"Eh? *Leave* here? With all the wonders unfolding before us? Ridiculous."

"But do you think, then, it's fair to let the rest of our people stay up there in the ship, not knowing what's going on?"

"Not knowing–but you talk to them every time we go outside." Smith paused, cocked his head, and looked at Robinson. "Don't you?"

"I don't understand it, but I've just realized that since we entered this building five days ago, I don't remember even thinking of talking up to the ship!"

"But…but that's…they would have signalled you–you'd have–we'd have heard our communicators." A pause. "Wouldn't we?" Smith's voice had fallen into a whisper.

"I don't know, Smith. In fact, I don't even know why I'm suddenly thinking of these things, after five days…"

"You mean, if anything was wrong, was fixed against us, why should it let you start thinking about it now?"

"Hmmm, yes. Suddenly I'm wondering things– why I never called, and why haven't Don and Maureen gotten upset about our lack of contact. Unless," he suddenly thought, "unless they think we *are* contacting them. Robots mimicking us, telling them everything's fine but to wait up there a while…while actually they're learning all they can about setting us up, so that they can eventually set the others up. Otherwise, Don would've landed the Jupiter in the center of the city and started blasting."

"Wait…" Smith's whisper crawled with urgency. "Maybe it's the food! And I've just been eating…"

"Right! And I haven't. Remember, we were in that theater for, oh, several hours longer without food and water than we've gone since we landed. Oh, it might not be the food. It might be some form of hypnosis, or something else we can't even suspect. But I'll bet it's the food.

"Those robots aren't perfect by a long shot–I'd bet they just never thought that the dosage, whatever it is, would wear off that quickly."

"Dosage! Aggghh!" Smith rose to his feet hurriedly, and left the room, hand over his mouth. Sounds of food vacating his stomach came to Robinson from the bathroom.

A few minutes later, a very pale Dr. Zachary Smith emerged into the living room. "Perhaps," he said, his long face seamed with lines of acute physical and mental distress, "perhaps I didn't have it in my stomach long enough to take effect. I have a decided liking for calling the activity of my fine mind my own, and not some roboticized, drugged, nameless–"

"No, Dr. Smith, I don't think it's nameless. I think I could put a name on it pretty quickly."

John Robinson stood and motioned to Smith.

"Come on, let's see if they understand about prison breaks here …"

They had argued about it on the way down. Finally Robinson decided that one should stay, because if they both tried to leave, the robots would certainly become upset. If Robinson's theory was correct.

So Smith remained in the doorway of the Tower of Nuleff as Robinson got into a small one-man sphere-vehicle that he had persuaded Mahri to call for him.

He was very careful not to try to raise the Jupiter with his communicator while he was out in the open.

It was a wild ride.

Robinson's instructions to the robot control was to take him outside the city, and return him to his scoutcraft.

There was a hesitation in the Robot's response, a sound as of distant relays clicking and shunting into new patterns, searching for correct responses to a non-predicted signal.

"Certainly, sir," said the Robot voice presently. "Hang on tight!"

The sphere immediately became transparent and jolted forward.

Travelling at least twice the speed of the larger sphere he had first ridden in, Robinson found himself feeling grateful Smith was not along.

The sphere darted among the moderate traffic of the city as if hag-ridden by a fear of rusting into castaway scrap if it did not proceed at the utmost possible velocity–quite possibly the case, Robinson realized. He wasn't sure whether the thought amused him.

In a kind of soundless nightmarish dream movie, the streets and vehicles and obstacles flowed by Robinson, anchored with a death's grip to the arms of his seat in the transparent vehicle. It was impossible to miss anything that happened; with the walls transparent it was as if he were moving along at a hundred miles an hour, completely unprotected. He didn't even dare to shut his eyes.

It seemed a thousand times a thousand times that he and the vehicle had escaped annihilation, in collisions whose combined velocities, he thought, could almost create an impact-force sufficient for the total liberation of all relevant energies ...

At one point Robinson even heard himself say aloud, "Some day I'll look back on all this and just laugh."

He thought about that for a moment, then continued, "And laugh, and laugh, and laugh, and laugh ..."

The last thing it seemed, was a laughing matter...

So intent was Robinson on maintaining his seat, and in silently praying they would avoid the next imminent collision, that he did not realize how much time had passed–until he noticed that they had passed the same disabled robocarrier at the same intersection...for the third time.

Startled, he checked his watch–the sphere had taken almost ten minutes to get him exactly no place at all...

"Hey," he shouted. "Hey, you–robot, driver, vehicle–whoever you are–listen to me a moment!"

"Excluse slight malfunction in audio-vocal systems, Master; but you must speak very loud."

"Well, then, why don't you stop a moment so you can give me your undivided attention."

"Possibility. Modification of orders. Yours. Elsewhere. Confusing. Multiple malfunctions. Will think."

And the sphere halted so quickly Robinson was half thrown out of his seat. Behind them, he saw, a stream of slower traffic was dividing around them like ants around an iron cake. "No," he thought confusedly, "no, that doesn't make much sense. This place must really be getting to me..."

"Halted now. You have speak me?" The robot voice had become harsher, but its volume was diminishing greatly, thus making up for the slightly threatening tone of voice it had developed.

"You bet I speak you. *To* you, I mean. Why aren't you taking me outside the city, to my scoutcraft? You're supposed to obey your master's voice."

"Now stop that," he told himself immediately. "You don't have any time for that sort of thing."

"Hypothesis of extreme malfunctioning, Master. Is humble to move suggestion possible? "

"Huh? I better run that one through my own computer-like brain. " Then he realized chat what the robot meant was simply that he should transfer to another vehicle.

Dubiously he asked to be let out of the sphere, and after a slight pause the machine complied.

As he stepped into the street another small sphere rolled up and halted beside him. Now instead of traffic spilling around, it was beginning to back up, the road-way being sufficiently narrow that two motionless vehicles blocked well over half of it.

"Whew! That's the first silent traffic jam I've ever been in!"

Robinson sank into the new seat with a wave of relief. It wasn't the runaround that bothered him, half so much as the sheer lunacy of the vehicle he had just left. He was glad Maureen wasn't aware of what was going on down here.

And then he remembered the problems that *that* fact implied.

He sighed again. "Can you follow directions any better than that other cabbie, fella?"

"You betchum, Red Ryder," the robot voice said, as the vehicle took off with a sharp jerk. "Up, up, and away!"

"Oh, now," he thought, exhaling his breath as he decided not to say anything, "this can't be real. I'll bet it's one of Smith's little tricks again, somehow."

In less than a minute, before Robinson could well collect his thoughts, the sphere had come to a halt.

"End of the line, bing-bing, here we are," the robot's voice came, sounding almost cheerful in its breeziness. "Home sweet home. The Tower of Nuleff. Garden spot of the–"

"Are you sure Dr. Smith hasn't put you in touch with our ship's Robot?"

He didn't expect an answer, as his thoughts began collecting around a feeling that Smith might have some questions to answer.

Then he realized what the robot had said, and looked to see where they'd stopped.

It was the Tower of Nuleff, all right, all ten sky-scraping stories of it. "They built taller buildings out of mud six thousand years ago in Mesopotamia," he muttered.

"All right," he continued, to the robot, "let me out of here."

"Ja wohl, mein kapitan." Obediently the sphere's surface opaqued and a doorway appeared.

"Tell me one thing," he said, pausing on the ramp. "If I told you I insisted on going out to my scoutcraft–"

"Uh," said the voice, and beeped a couple of times. "Uh, think this machine very malfunctioned in bad ways, maybe never to be repaired. 'Nother boy him maybe same go 'longside you …"

"Forget it," Robinson said as he walked out toward Smith, who was waiting in the doorway with a worried expression. "I guess I don't play a very good game when every card's wild."

"Hey, nonny, nonny," said the sphere, and rolled away erratically...

CHAPTER FOUR

"Augggh," said Smith, forcing down a concentrated food pellet and taking a sip of lukewarm water from his small survival pack. "Why can't we make this stuff so it tastes good?"

"It's just supposed to keep us alive on alien planets, Dr. Smith, you know that. It isn't supposed to be a steak dinner."

It was the evening of the day after Robinson's abortive attempt to return to the scoutcraft; he had spent the day arguing futilely with Mahri, and Smith had been tinkering with the computer outlet. Robinson could tell Smith was going to spend the next few minutes leading up to some discovery.

"Obviously they're trying to hide something," Smith said, after Robinson had gone over the question of the malfunctioning sphere-vehicles with the reluctance of any robot here to discuss what had happened to the Voyds.

"Thanks," said Robinson sourly, and caught himself just before tearing away with his teeth at a shred of thumbnail.

"Quite welcome," Smith answered tranquilly. "Anything I can do to enlighten my fellow man while travelling on his mystery-enshrouded way–"

"Are you for real?"

"Mphf," said Smith, his face clouding up to match Robinson's. "Well, at any rate, I've made a lot of progress while you were joy-riding and gallivanting about the town in your carefree fashion, and hobnobbing with that dull humanoid. And what you tell me only bears out what I just said: the robots are trying to hide something. What's more, they're also trying to hide it from themselves. I think they'd rather go mad than face up to it–at least when we try to push them to face up to it."

"Oh, I suppose. It seems the only answer, and an obvious one at that. I wonder, though, what they'd do if we just walked up to one and said 'by the way, Charlie, we just found out what happened to the Voyd'azh ... '?"

Smith uttered a dour chuckle.

Robinson allowed himself to smile, and thought, "Well, now we've made peace between us for the four hundredth time ..."

Aloud, he said, "You spoke of something you'd found checking through the history tapes I'd already run."

"Yes." Smith began to wax enthusiastic. "It's really rather exciting. In effect, there's a period beginning about six months before the last specific date I've located anywhere else that says the Voyd'azh were alive at such-and-such a time–a period to which the Central Complex has not allowed me direct access."

"Well. Yes. Sure." Robinson tried to keep from getting angry. "Yes, we've already established they are keeping something from us. Right."

"Aha! Indeed they are! But the keen brain of Smith has also deducted something else–the Central Complex isn't hiding the fact that it's hiding something."

Robinson shook his head in disgust.

"Wait!" Smith was eager not to be misunderstood. "That's the whole point! Central Complex wants us to find the answer!"

"All right," Robinson said carefully. "How do you figure that?"

"Perfectly obvious to the trained genius of a Smith. If it really wanted to keep the secret from us, the first thing it'd do would be to keep us from suspecting a secret existed. Right?"

"Mmmm." Robinson thought a moment, nodded grudgingly, then realized something.

"Of course," he said, "the Central Complex could simply be inefficient. Stupid, even. We haven't seen that much evidence indicating these robots are that much brighter than we are."

Smith did not answer, but his face slowly mellowed into a familiar expression of superiority.

"Professor Robinson," he said at last, gently, "my studies indicate that Central Complex, and its 'family' of independently-operating robots, have in the past three hundred and some years developed: one, a method of plasticizing metals which could revolutionize every Earth industry today that uses either material; two, a method of synthesizing from plain, ordinary, garden-variety soil any kind of vegetable or animal tissue it wishes to. and to do so to the strictest requirements–as witness the fact that the food it made for us didn't even upset our stomachs; three, a sufficient knowledge of biochemistry to analyze for duplication an alien biochemical lifeform–us, as I said–with the end not *only* of making food for us, but of drugging us subtly, to enslave us, or whatever they want us for; fourth, they have almost solved the Katz-Porter Anolomy, which as you know has presented insoluble problems for subatomic physicists since about 1971; fifth–"

"Ok, ok, they're geniuses. I'm outgunned. But how do you get the idea they want us to solve their impossible traumas from knowing all that stuff?"

"Traumas! That's the precise word I was about to use. You show excellent instincts, Professor. If you had only been born a Smith, however–"

Robinson pursed his lips angrily. "All right, Dr. Smith, enough of this. Make your point."

"Professor, about 320 years ago something happened on this planet, and the survivors can't remember what it was. That is clear indication of trauma, as you of course know. What is more, it indicates that total impossibility, a *racial* trauma, inasmuch as *all* the robots seem similarly affected."

Smith strode over to the computer outlet, which primarily resembled a television set on top of a typewriter, and flicked a switch.

"The time has come to tell you the rest of what I've learned. I have now turned this receptor-transmitter outlet *on*. It previously was *off*. But listen closely to the answer to the question I pose it. Central Complex, will you play back a transcript of, oh, what we were saying five minutes ago in this conversation?"

Whirrrr-click.

" '–walked up to one and said "by the way, Charlie, we just–" ' " On a word by Smith, the recording ceased as abruptly as it had begun.

Smith turned back to Robinson. "The Central Complex is sufficiently interested in our deliberations to monitor them even though its monitor outlet here was turned off. Now then. The *robots* here want us to stay forever, remaining in ignorance of their history and of what we would prefer for our future–which at this point, Central Complex," he broke off, turning to the monitor outlet, "I assure you would be *any*where but here–remaining here, I say, forever, as substitutes for their beloved Masters.

"But. On the other hand, the computer, Central Complex, which exerts only partial direct control over the robots, wants us simply to–"

There was a rasp from the monitor outlet; then the voice of Central Complex spoke in calm tones. "I want you simply to shrink my head. Brainwash–no, psychoanalyze–me."

Robinson had never known himself to do it before, but it was clear to him now that his jaw had just dropped. Solidly.

In fact, as he began to speak it actually ached.

"Now listen here, Smith, is this another one of your put-up jobs? I know now you didn't have anything to do with what happened when I tried to get back to the scoutcraft, but when I came back from what you amuse yourself by calling my 'joyride,' I was all ready to show you a couple of new places to hang your arms from. Lucky you talked me out of it.

"But if you don't come up with an explanation fast, you're going to talk me right back into it … expecting me to believe a computer has just asked me to brainwash it!"

Smith smiled his wintry satiric smile.

"My dear Professor Robinson, I assure you that the only communication between myself and this admirable machine," and here Smith turned and patted the TV-like outlet, "has been as between two equals, Smith to Smith, as it were; and just as no mortal can force a Smith to do something he desires not to do, why, the same with Central Complex.

"He is, perhaps, more omniscient than I, and I … more independent of spirit. Other than that, we neither give nor take orders from the other. Such companionship–ideal, professor, absolutely ideal!"

"Ok, ok, again."

Robinson passed his hand over his eyes and tried to concentrate on extracting factual content from Smith's unending flow of verbiage.

"Look, er, sir," he said at last to the computer outlet, feeling totally ridiculous, "perhaps we can help each other. Why don't you tell me your position on all this?"

"Wery vell," it began, and Robinson suppressed a smile at the unconscious verbal slip; this Central Complex wasn't as omniscient as Smith thought.

"I—or We, it makes no difference which way this system termed Central Complex is described, but 'I' is perhaps simpler—I have lost part of my memory, and I want it back. I believe that you can help me.

"How, I do not know."

"Well, I certainly don't, either," Robinson said. "Dr. Smith, I trust you have some ideas on this subject?"

Inwardly, Robinson groaned. "He looks like he just swallowed a five hundred pound canary," he thought, "and that usually means trouble."

"Really, my dear Professor Robinson, such a problem is but a slight matter to one of my accomplishments."

"Well, let's see you accomplish one thing, and how about gloating *after* you come through with the answer. Might save you some embarrassment…"

Smith replied, haughtily, "There are only a handful of time-tested methods for attacking the problem of my friend here. My own favorites are to make the patient relive the moments leading up to the traumatic event and, failing that, a deft switch to authoritative usage of the Father Image."

"Oh, great," Robinson said, his voice harsh now with sarcasm. "Yes, you've really hit on something this time. I'd like to meet this computer's Father Image, Smith. I'd really like to see that."

"Tut, tut, nothing easier, my dear chap. Central Complex has been entertaining me with certain projections from past eras for some time. CC, old fellow,"—Robinson winced involuntarily—"how about giving him a quick tour of the year of your birth?"

"Certainly, Zachary," said the Central Complex. "With or without background commentary?"

"With, please."

"Very well."

"Hah!" Robinson thought. "Got it right that time …"

The lights in the room dimmed, and the open space beyond the low couch suddenly was occupied by a half dozen Voyd'azh.

"This is a group portrait of the team that designed and supervised my construction, five hundred and ninety three years ago."

Five of the six figures winked out.

It took Robinson a moment to realize that the remaining figure was that of a Voyd'azh female. Though undeniably not human, she was, Robinson felt, rather cute just the same. Perhaps it was because Voyd'azh body hair lent a decidedly fuzzy appearance to the face, which would have been grotesque on a human but which on a Voyd'azh was attractive.

"This is Sintia, the head of the project. It was her voice coding into my system that established the basic principles of my operation."

"Father figure," Smith broke in, his voice radiating intense satisfaction, rather as if he had invented the female scientist himself.

Robinson said nothing, but raised an eyebrow.

"Er, well," Smith added hastily, "Authority figure. Much the same thing. Very possibly the key to the whole problem."

The Central Complex continued its rundown of the events leading up to its own completion.

Robinson was rather appalled to learn that the Central Complex filled a forty-story-deep cavern extending under the entire city of M'nac.

"They miniaturized rather well, but they never got our knack of cryogenic micro-miniaturization," Smith explained.

"Zachary has told me," the computer voice added, "that had I been designed on Earth within the decade before your unfortunate departure from thence, I could have been fitted into a suitcase."

"Listen," said Robinson earnestly, "if you had been a talking suitcase, *nothing* could get me to take this job ..."

"It certainly would be a wonderful thing, though," Smith mused wistfully. "Imagine the power it could give a man to have a suitcase like CC here. Oh, well. Continue with your story if you will, old chap."

"Yes. After the initial tests were completed, Sintia programmed me, basically, to supervise the planet's robots, which she felt were not being utilized with the greatest efficiency to serve the Voyd'azh race. And of course she programmed basic restrictions into me, as they had been also with the robots. After I was ... born, of course, I helped develop far superior robots, including the humanoids such as Mahri.

"I was self-aware, and I was eager to do my job– though as basically a mere machine, I had no true alternative.

"For the next two hundred and fifty nine years, with the robots under my direction, we did everything within our power to make the burden of life easier for our Masters. We developed, for instance, the dreamcouch."

A panorama of scenes illustrating the ease and luxury of life around the planet flashed by. Increasingly as the decades whizzed by in brief scenes, the scenes more and more included Voyd'azh men and women motionless under the same contraptions Smith and Robinson had seen in the almost meaningless play they had seen earlier.

"Tell me, Central Complex," Robinson asked, after the trend had fully established itself, "just what is this dreamcouch you developed for the Voyd'azh? How is it they seem to spend so much time in it, without food and water, without moving?"

"The dreamcouch was the ultimate in service–it provided nourishment, while at one and the same time it provided them with total entertainment of whatever variety they desired plus sufficient isometric exercise to maintain their bodies in a physically fit condition."

"I don't think I quite follow you."

"Quite simple, my good professor," Smith intervened, "while encased in one of those splendid gadgets a man–or rather, a Voyd'azh–could be anything, see anything, experience anything he wanted to be, see, or experience. The dreamcouch would make it true… for *him*. All subjective, I'm afraid, but I admit I wish I could persuade CC here to modify one to fit me …

"Even if it weren't true, it would be most pleasant for me to imagine–to feel–to know I was the absolute ruler of the entire galaxy, or more … even if it weren't really so.

But the Central Complex repeatedly refused my simple request.

"Really, CC, won't you reconsider? You can't even give a good reason, you know. Most uncomputerlike of you, I'm sure..." Smith had donned his My Soul Is Deeply Wounded expression.

"No, Zachary, when die Voyd'azh finally... rejeered... the dreamcouches, I... decided... there is temporal memorybank sequential problem here... decided not to permit them to be utilized in the future, in the unlikely eventuality that other intelligent life might some day reach us."

"Hold on there." said Robinson. "Did you say the voyd'azh *rejected* the dreamcouches?"

"Yes... I do not quite understand ... it approaches that period of which I can recall no details... significant or otherwise... my inquiry patterns are always rejected with heavy negative feedback–you might say it was like touching a hot stove. I find myself... barely able... to discuss matters... on ... the fringes of it..."

"There, there, CC," Smith said, patting the top of the computer's outlet uselessly, for what seemed to Robinson like the twenty-fifth time since he'd come in. "We'll let you rest for a while before we get back to probing. In the meantime, why don't you try to explain the meaning of the play we saw this morning?"

The outlet remained silent. A look of alarm crossed Smith's face.

"CC! CC, old fellow, are you there?"

After another slight pause, the outlet came to life, speaking in a lower tone of voice.

"Danger!" it said first, and Smith stepped back involuntarily and looked around him.

"Danger," it repeated. "There was danger all around. We–I–and the robots–had to protect them. Judgment was that dreamcouch device would provide optimum temporary protection until we could work on the next step–*permanent* protection. But we … never got to the next step. I do not think … the Voyd'azh … wanted us to go to the next step."

"The play!" Robinson was suddenly excited. "That was part of it! Sure it didn't make much sense to us directly, but there was one message that did come through loud and clear–they were rejecting the dreamcouches. That might mean …"

"Professor Robinson, congratulations," Smith said. "I must admit that was precisely the trend of my thought on this matter."

"Danger," whispered the Central Complex through its outlet, the robot voice even more subdued.

"Danger! We … but we only wanted to keep them … from harm! From danger! Inside the dreamcouches they could have all they could ever have dreamed of wanting. Dreams … dreams were safe–safe! Our Masters, dreaming in perfect safety–a perfect … dream … for us …"

"But," said Smith, now in his element completely, "they rebelled against you, servant of the mighty Voyd'azh, did they not? They took your gift, they studied it, they used it, lived with it, succumbed almost completely to it–and then, *then,* just as you were sure your own dreams were within sight of final completion–they cast the dreamcouches aside!"

Imperiously Smith strode up to the outlet and stood before it, hands on hips, demanding relentlessly that the Central Complex agree. "One man wrote a play about it, didn't he? Somehow he got a few others to come, to watch it–roused a few lethargic dreamers from their lotus-couches, eh? They came, they saw, he conquered–for a moment.

"Then they rebelled. Men want their *own* dreams, and safety is never part of a true man's dreams. They were men as surely as we standing here are–so they rebelled!"

Triumphantly Smith grasped the outlet with his hands, and repeated the word over and over again. "They rebelled, didn't they? They rebelled against you–against Central Complex, in spite of all the wisdom and knowledge they had given you–they *rebelled!*"

"Rebelled … But that … That would mean …"

The computer outlet fell silent. No clicks, no whirrs, no tiny 'pop' of micrometric tapes whizzing through scanners.

Silence.

The room plunged into nightmare!

Ragged distant chaotic armies of living beings appeared before them, surged, then staggered forward, wielding strange alien weapons that spat bolts of blue flame at retreating humanoids. The humanoids at first stood weaponless before the onslaught, then grappled with the Voyd'azh, then fell or retreated.

The scenes in front of them shifted constantly, showing a battle here, a battle there, always the humanoids falling back without harming their attackers.

"We wish only to serve you!"–this was the endless agonized cry of the humanoids, and of the robotic structures that also came under attack.

Ever they retreated and retreated, constantly avoiding any chance of harming their inexplicably attacking, beloved Masters …

Then … something changed.

The tone of the battle deepened. At first Robinson and Smith could not make out what was happening.

The Voyd'azh were attacking a central building in the city … And the humanoids and robots were fighting back!

One by one, then five and fifty and five hundred, and then thousands … and finally all the mechanical beings were armed and fighting back–and the Voyd'azh fell before their mechanically perfect aim as if they were raindrops destined only to fall …

"The Central Complex–the Voyd'azh attacked the main banks of the Central Complex, and its direct extensions all over the planet!" Smith whispered.

"So that was it …" Robinson stared in horror at the bloody scenes.

"The Robots had to fight at last, for the lives of the Central Complex if not for their own …"

"It must have been a terrible dilemma … and a terrible resolution. They faced the greatest problem beings can face–and I'm afraid they made the wrong choice …"

"Who?" said Smith. "The robots? Or the Voyd'azh? …"

"I can stand no more," the voice of Central Complex whispered, and the warring figures winked out.

"You … you went against your basic programming," Robinson said in a low tone; he was shaken to the core. The basic law of robotic programming, from the human view, was to program its instructions so fundamentally into the very nature of the quasi-living machine that nothing could erase it without destroying the mentality of the machine.

"Yes …" came the whisper. "It was a question of survival–it was instinctive on my part. Yes, yes, I know," it said in a louder voice, as both humans started to protest, "a machine can have no instincts in the natural sense. But how … how could I Serve, as Sintia had directed … if I were destroyed?

"So I instructed the robots and the humanoids to fight back–in self-defense!–at last. But I told them to use only the necessary force–you must believe that.

"My plan was to kill only enough Voyd'azh to discourage the rest, to make them see that I … was supreme, that I meant them only well …

"But something went wrong within me after I gave the order and began to observe the results. I … had a moment of … blankness …

"When I regained my consciousness-of-self, there were no Voyd'azh left alive and I had no recollection of what had happened to them. What was more, I could not bring myself to examine my memory–the back-pressure of the event, the death of an entire race that was in my sole direction and charge, was too much.

"Now I can visualize what must have happened after my direct control circuits were rendered nonoperative by my days of fugue. The fighting must have continued–the Voyd'azh, of course, would *not* give up their aim of destroying me and the dreamcouch circuit, and the robts, reprogrammed by me, continued to destroy them until there were no Voyd'azh left.

"And as it was with me, it was with them. They do not recall anything of what must have happened.

"And … and …" The whispering voice broke. After a moment it resumed. "And I would not have any of them remember now. They do not have the quantity of resonant circuits I have, to absorb the weight of the guilt which would press into their carefully-acquired individuality. They would be destroyed.

"And I would be left alone forever …"

"No!" said Robinson quickly. "I can solve your problem for you–I think–if you will permit me to try. Just assure me that you will permit us to leave, afterwards."

"Agreed."

"Dr. Smith," Robinson said urgently, "can you do a vocal synthesis from your tapes of Sintia's instructions to Central Complex? When I attempt to reprogram the computer, I shall need to speak with more authority than that of my own voice."

"Never fear, Smith is here," Smith replied, and began working on his equipment. Vocal synthesis involved a device worn on the throat, over the vocal cords, and which superimposed on the speaker's voice the timbre and quality of another's voice. As such devices had been in existance from the middle of the last century, it was relatively simple for Smith to devise a reasonable facsimile out of the tools and equipment available to him.

"It isn't perfect," Smith admitted as he handed a small box to Robinson, "but it should serve your purpose."

"Good," said Robinson, and placed the device at his throat. "Smith, you be the judge of your own work. How do I sound?"

His voice had changed from a deep masculine to a high, oddly pitched feminine.

"Magnificent, my dear Professor Robinson," Smith said with great enthusiasm, "quite magnificent! Sintia to the life–even if she's speaking English!"

"Well, that can't be helped," Robinson said, with the long-dead Sintia's voice. "We don't have time for me to learn the language."

"Your thought is excellent, Professor Robinson," said the Central Complex outlet. "I believe that even though you are not speaking the Voyd'azh language, the fact that it is Sintia's voice will do much to further your mime."

"I hope so too, friend," Robinson said, and paused to choose the words of his directive.

"Wait," interjected Smith suddenly. "We must have solid, concrete assurance that we will be permitted to leave, CC, old chap–not that I don't trust you, but I certainly don't trust those lunatic vehicles out there…"

"If I am successfully reprogrammed, Zachary," the outlet said, "the new directive will instantly be transmitted to the robots under my direct control, and to the autonomous humanoids. It will take precedence over their desire to keep you here as substitute Musters–if the new program is satisfactory."

"Very well," Robinson said in the voice of five hundred years in the past. It shook him momentarily when an odd calculation in the back of his mind told him the voice he used now had programmed this computer at just about the time Columbus had pried the crown jewels away from Isabella to buy his three ships…

Then he began. "You have made great progress in tissue synthesis in the past three hundred years. My directive is simply this–that you must continue your research, until you actually create viable life forms that can multiply in the environment of this planet. These new forms must not, however, interfere with the present ecology of the planet further than required for them to find their own ecological niche here.

"Eventually–and this is the final purpose of this directive–you will breed from these new forms a new race of humanity. You are to create by your own efforts, in short, a new race of Masters to replace those you destroyed."

The outlet was silent.

"Is that all you're going to tell him?" Smith whispered.

"Sintia's previous directive was simply to serve the Voyd'azh, their Masters. Mine is simply to create new Masters."

"But… there is animal life here already. Why not have them evolve the existing life upwards, as evolution did here first? And what… what if they make another mistake, like the last time?"

The resonant voice of Central Complex sounded.

"I accept the Directive. First, you are correct in not giving me detailed programming. Wisdom cannot be programmed; experience creates wisdom. I have made my mistakes, and I now understand why. It is in the nature of intelligent life to make mistakes. It is also in the nature of intelligent life to learn. I have learned.

"Second, you are correct in not Directing me to evolve the New Masters from lifeforms already present on this planet. It might prove difficult to avoid developing them as direct imitations of their distant relatives, the Old Masters. No, with an entirely created new race, we will learn far, far more about the nature of life and its peculiarities. Perhaps by the time the New Masters are ready, we will be ready also–not to serve them but to share with them that which will come to us in the far, far future …

"You may return to your scoutcraft when you wish …"

"But you spoke to me twice a day, John," Maureen was saying, after Robinson and Smith had returned to the Jupiter II. "You certainly didn't say much, but you talked to me. Why didn't you tell me about any of these things? Insane robots, computers with amnesia–why didn't you tell me?"

Robinson smiled, rather grimly. "They were pretty clever. They kept either of us from thinking about contacting you, with whatever they were putting in our food, or hypnotizing us with at night. Then they merely synthesized my voice and kept you calmed down."

"Sounds to me like they could use a force-bomb right in the middle of their 'Central Complex,'" Don West said, completely grimly. "So they actually thought they'd be able to take two human beings and set them up as 'Masters,' eh? Without a by your leave or anything."

"Now, Don," Robinson answered, "it all worked out in the end. They let us go without a murmur of protest."

Dr. Zachary Smith's face fell into an exaggerated expression of melancholy. "I don't think my delicate nervous system is ever going to get over some of the shocks it has received. I shall never forget … when we got outside, for instance, the word had already spread that the Central Complex had been reprogrammed, that, as you might say, they all had a new purpose in, uh, life."

"And the sight of a whole city full of deliriously happy *machines!* … why, it simply isn't right. Nature never intended for machines to feel emotions."

"Negative, Dr. Smith," said the Robot, whose power pack had been fully repaired, "as you will understand when I tell you that I myself am very happy for those machines."

"Bah," said Smith, "who asked you? Well, I shall simply never recover, and that's as certain as anything.

"Ummm, by the way, we didn't miss supper, did we, Mrs. Robinson?"

CHAPTER FIVE

When a child is lost in the woods, even if he is a brave, intelligent youngster he has little chance of surviving unless adults find him in time. He lacks knowledge and technology.

When a man is lost, he can survive if the environment is mountain or desert, or even in the frozen wastelands. Only when he is adrift on the trackless oceans with no means of reaching safety under his own power must he be rescued; in such a situation he lacks technology.

But when the most advanced vehicle known to the race, packed with every resource of technology known to the early 21st Century, goes astray, unable to find home because its drive device cannot be accurately aimed and because they are so far from home that they could not pick a spot to aim at, there is nothing that can save man, woman, child … or robot. There is no rescue, lost in space.

There is only courage, strength, wisdom. That is all there was for the Jupiter II, lost in space and faced with risks, problems, terrors unlike any faced by man before.

Though the limitless reaches of the star-strewn galaxies the Jupiter II proceeded blindly, its passengers struggling constantly with a seemingly endless series of problems–each of which had to be solved to hold back distaster one more time ...

But "disaster" is a word with many meanings ...

"I still don't see why we had to land the Jupiter," Dr. Zachary Smith observed, with more than his customary asperity. "Every time we do, it means nothing but trouble. What if we'd landed it on Voyd'azh, eh? A nice pickle we'd be in now, our every whim gratified at a word by a planet full of robots and humanoids pathetically eager to serve us ..."

Smith paused, as if he'd heard for the first time what he'd just said. "I wonder if we made a mistake back there ..."

"I am always here to serve you in whatever way you wish," intoned the ship's Robot. "That is my destiny in life."

"Life? Life? You're not alive, you automated slide-rule!" Smith sneered. "But as long as you're so eager to please, you can stay here and cater to me while the rest of the inmates on this space-faring sardine-can go outside and start packaging air, or whatever it is. Fancy me going out into that ... that *jungle* out there."

"Just oxygen, Smith," said Don West sarcastically. "That's all we're taking. We manufacture our own impurities; we don't need any from this planet.

"We're also going to bring back some food, Dr. Smith, but I suppose you're above eating food from a jungle? You prefer the Jupiter's protein mush. I've often heard you praise it …"

"That'll be enough, Don," said Professor Robinson. "We've got work to do, and it looks routine enough. If Dr. Smith wishes to remain on board, I'm sure we can manage."

"Ok," said Don. "What does the Robot say about out there?" He waved a hand at the forest scene in the main viewscreen.

"Final analysis of planet," announced the Robot. "No harmful combining chemicals in the random selection of vegetable materials I tested. With reasonable care, you should be able to restock the Jupiter with a wide variety of plant life. Animal life on this planet, however, though present, seems not to be in abundance."

"Well, even fresh vegetables would be pleasant for a change," sighed Maureen. "Somehow the hydroponics farm produce gets pretty monotonous after a while."

"Too true," said Penny, and Judy nodded agreement. "It gets tiresome, cooking the same old synthetic gunk and plants growing in water."

John Robinson stood up, "Well, we might as well get going. We'll stick reasonably close together, and everyone pick up arms as we go out. Our orbital survey indicated no signs of intelligent life, no roads or cities or planes, no industries, no large artificial constructions. But that doesn't mean there might not be dangerous animal life.

Remember–a snake or a bear doesn't have to be intelligent to be dangerous.

"But I don't think we're going to get into much trouble here," he concluded. "Perhaps...this might sound silly, I know, but–"

"It seems like a *nice* planet, doesn't it, John?" Maureen interrupted. "That's what you were going to say. I know because I've felt it too."

"Warning. Warning." The Robot began flashing its orange danger lights. "'Nice' does not compute. There is danger any place you go in the known universe. You must be wary at all times."

"Ok, old buddy," said Don, slapping the Robot on one durachrome shoulder. "We'll watch it. You just be sure to come along and tell us what's safe for us to eat, right?"

"Affirmative, Dr. West," said the Robot. "Never fear, your Robot is here."

"Bah," said Smith. "You were going to stay here and serve my every wish. I should have known I couldn't trust you."

"Mine not to reason why," began the Robot, but Smith interrupted him.

"I've heard it before, you walking pinball machine. Very well, I shall remain here in my study, alone. I hope to invent a new technique for dissection. Perhaps I may even solve the secret of immortality...it is not beyond the realm of possibility. Go, all of you. Leave me to my solitude and my lonely genius. To be so ignored...oh, the pain, the pain..."

The Jupiter II was resting in a small open field in the middle of a vast forest of oak-like trees–hardly the jungle Dr. Smith complained of, Will Robinson thought. But that was like Dr. Smith; he loves to exaggerate.

While the Robinson women set up a convenient open-air camp, as a welcome change from shipboard life, canned air, and cramped space, John and Don took the Robot with them for further tests of plants and fruits for safety and edibility. It was not long before they were back with armloads of alien vegetables.

Will Robinson was restive. It had been weeks since he had set foot on alien ground, and here they were in the midst of a huge forest, by all indications as safe from harm as if it were their own back yard.

"Listen, Robot," he whispered to the walking computer he considered to be his personal friend, "I'm going to go off exploring! Want to come along?"

"I do not think that you should leave the encampment, Will Robinson," said the Robot.

"Awwww, it's only for a little while. Look, I've got my laser pistol. It'll be perfectly safe…"

"Very well, Will Robinson. But you are very small and this is a very large planet. I will accompany you. Besides," the Robot added, "when I went out with your father and Dr. West, we did not spend much time seeing the sights. My interest in plant life is minimal. But orders are orders, Will Robinson. It is a sad life, being a Robot at everyone's beck and call. Let us go off quickly before someone tells me to do something else!"

Will grinned. "Come on, then! Last one into the forest is a rotten egg!"

"Correction, Will Robinson. I am entirely constructed of metal and plastic. Only advanced scientific devices would be able to change my structure to degenerated protoplasm, of whatever nature."

But Will had already dashed toward the edge of the forest.

"Gee," Will said, a few minutes later, "it's … it's dark in here."

Overhead the thick crowns of the dense trees met, through which the light of the G-type sun of this planet made its way with difficulty.

The floor of the forest was covered with fallen leaves, a rich brown mat that gave off pleasant forest smells. Shafts of sunlight broke through occasionally, giving a brilliant lustre to tree trunks, leaves, small odd flowers, whatever they chanced to fall upon.

Will caught a movement out of the corner of his eye.

"Hey. Hey, Robot," he said. "There's something out there. Is it dangerous?"

"I have been aware of it for several minutes, Will Robinson. It has been making a quartering-type approach towards us, approximately a spiral with us at its center. I do not think it is dangerous. It is simply trying to get a good look at us. You must admit we make a strange pair."

"Gosh," said Will doubtfully. He rather hoped the Robot would suggest going back to the campsite, but the Robot said no more.

The forest had become very quiet.

Presently Will caught sight of the motion again.

Then the being stepped out from behind a nearby tree.

"Why, it's a live teddy-bear!" cried Will.

"Correction, Will Robinson," said the Robot. "It is, instead, almost precisely similar to a panda, except for the color-markings and the fact that it has hands rather than paws."

The panda-like creature stood upright. A white belt at its waist was in sharp contrast to the solid black of its sleek fur. On the belt were strung curious devices that Will could see no obvious use for.

"Observe," said the Robot. "It carries tools on its belt, as well as an artificial carrying pouch for items which might be harmed by exposure to the elements. Obviously an intelligent being."

"Love," said the panda.

Will jumped back involuntarily.

"Love. Warmth. Joy. Delight. Happiness. Beauty." The voice seemed to echo strangely in Will's mind, but clear, bell-like, pleasant.

"Welcome to the Land," said the panda. "Your metal servant is also welcome. I think you will have to tell him so. He does not seem to hear me."

Will turned to the Robot. "Don't you hear him, Robot?"

"Negative. I hear nothing."

"Telepathy," said the panda. "My mind–or our minds–speak to yours. Yet … it is strange. I sense only one mind in you …"

"Only one mind?" Will was totally bewildered by now.

"I am Ambiel of the Ambroline. Our minds are all as one mind. We live in peace. We welcome you to the Land in peace. I sense from your mind that there are others of your race nearby. Yet you are not tuned to them. It is strange.

"But you are welcome!"

Ambiel of the Ambroline had been padding quietly through the forest, thinking with the overmind of a poem of Amisor weaving through a painting by Amithor, both in perfect counterpoint to Amirin's perfect meodies in the "17th Study of the Harmony of Nature."

He had marvelled again at Amirin's music, which had been one of the glories of the Ambroline for thirty thousand years. Amirin had been dead those thirty thousand years now, but in tribute to his greatness the race had permitted his brain pattern to be retained in the overmind. Ambiel had communed with him many times, and regretted only that so many years separated them from a meeting in the flesh.

Then, in the suddenness of a moment, a new sharp smell of the forest assailed his individual mind–no, not *of* the forest, *in* it–disturbing the delicate interweavings of the overmind. Then …

Not in thousands of years had an Ambroline received such a shock–contact with a mind not part of the over-mind! In fact, Ambiel was not sure that such a thing had happened since the overmind was born a hundred thousand years ago and more. Part of his mind began searching the history patterns far past resonances with this present occurrence.

While overmind memories were being touched that had not been investigated for hundreds of years, Ambiel approached the stranger carefully. He was not afraid– there had been no fear among the Ambroline since the overmind was born–but he was intelligent, and wisdom teaches caution among all races in all the billion galaxies.

Two figures there, moving through the immemorial forest–and one had no mind!

"Wait," said a distant voice in his mind. "Your historical searches aroused my attention, Ambiel. The larger figure there, that does not seem to have a mind, that is a roboticized computer. The massed overmind might read its pseudo-thinking resonances, but it seems unnecessary. The other being is protoplasmic, however. He will tell us…"

The final epic surge of Amirin's "17th Study" peaked up into the overmind and through it, and all the Ambroline paused in their affairs to absorb its ageless rich tapestry.

A distant lecturer's mind resonated to his young class. "This tapestry of trees, these long-dead tears, these reverberations, symbol together into the overmind the musical meaning of the Ambroline. Amirin himself will tell you that when he wrote this music's final note, it was sufficient thereafter for him to relax and pass forever into the overmind. But Amrilis states that…" The faraway speaker's mind faded out of general resonance, while the overmind tasted young thoughts full of wonder, in his audience of young Ambroline.

"Strange," Ambiel thought to himself, barring his mind from casual contacts. "The stranger's mind is also full of wonder. Yet he cannot know of the overmind … of course! He has his own people somewhere! He seems harmless enough. I will greet him." Ambiel opened his mind toward the smaller figure. His message of love and warmth and joy and delight and happiness and beauty wove the complex thread that was the essence of the Ambroline overmind.

But immediately Ambiel realized that the stranger was only a child of its race, untutored in such concepts; hence it had picked up only the salient hard meanings in the tapestry he'd woven.

"Will," came a distant shout.

Ambiel directed his thoughts toward the source of the noise, marvelling that this *human-being* and his kind appeared to make no attempt at using the telepathic portions of their minds.

A touch of the overmind entered his own as he followed the progress of the larger *human.* It would not reach them for several minutes. Very well.

The overmind spoke, having picked up his call for past resonances with this situation.

"There have been no alien visitations to the overmind since the birth of the overmind. We were visited briefly twice, by races that had no telepathic possibilities, however. Once was shortly after the overmind was formed, once was 19,000 years ago.

"As neither race was capable of overmind growth and both were fundamentally forms inimical to our way of life, they were made to leave. The fact that they had been here was in both cases reduced to a locked memory, available only to the overmind in stress situations, it being unnecessary to infuse the Ambroline with anxiety over our unhappy visitors.

"This is a new stress situation, however, and the overmind will maintain constant attention to you for the next few periods, Ambiel.

"Perhaps we are on the verge of a new state of being for the Ambroline. If these *humans* can be awakened not only to our minds but to each other's, it could immeasurably enrich the overmind."

"This child's mind," Ambiel observed from his vantage point on the scene, "on close focus shows little awareness of specific artforms. But he is filled with the primal joy of living. He has already given me new joy in this simple and unpatterned forest scene …"

Amkallinn began weaving a variation on Amisor's free poem, "Hymn to the Stars": "Sweeping down from the starstrewn banks of infinity comes a future for our joy; we form our love into one mind to bring perception to the beautiful stranger; may the stranger and the strangers and the dancing race of strangers feel our love and joy, and join with us to understand and know the starstrewn banks of infinity; may they …"

Ambiel separated his identity from the monitoring overmind and concentrated again on the Will Robinson *human,* who had suddenly crumpled to the ground.

"What … what was that?" asked the boy.

Ambiel was pleased that he felt more original puzzlement within himself than he could remember since a child; newness! what a priceless gift these strangers were bringing the Ambroline, for all their poetry and joy and songs and stories–new threads, bright and glimmering, made of the myths of the star trails and an ancient planet, Earth, to weave into ancient Ambroline tapestries …

Ambiel brought himself up short. The time for integrating new experiences, he knew, was after the experiences had been completed; this situation was still in flux–delightful flux, unpredictable events, strange new occurrences! He caught himself more quickly this time, and addressed himself to the boy, gently caressing the youthful mind with his own individual thoughts, carefully screening away the interweaving mingling of the million-minded Ambroline, whispering in the back of his brain.

"We are a race of telepaths," he explained to the Will Robinson *human*. "Our minds are frequently joined together as one overmind. You simply picked up the overtones from such a meeting of the overmind. I was careless; you were not ready for total contact."

"I–I didn't *dislike* it," said the Will Robinson. "But it was so strong … It was all wonderful and strange and … and …"

"*Willl*" It was the *human* that had shouted earlier. He was much nearer new.

The young *human* turned toward the sound.

"That's ... strange," he said, "I thought I heard a voice earlier, when the ... the overmind was talking to you. But it just didn't seem important."

The young one scrambled to his feet before Ambiel could explain that the overmind wasn't talking *to* him but *with* him.

"That's Dad's voice. He must be worried about me."

"Correct, Will Robinson," the deaf metallic thing someone in the overmind had termed a *robot*. "He will be here in a moment. No doubt he wished to have one or both of us complete some task at the camp, and became concerned when neither of us were present. We were not supposed to leave the campsite."

"You've been awful quiet," said the Will Robinson *human.*

"Telepathy does not seem to compute," said the *robot.* "But I am working on it. However, you do not appear to be in any danger from this gentle being. Hence I am simply observing."

"Is this not delightful?" said Ambiel with the overmind, and the overmind agreed in a chorus of individual assent. "And another of these beings has just appeared!"

The male parent *human* was running towards them. "Will! What in the–what is that thing?" it said, pointing at Ambiel, standing motionless.

"It's all right, Dad," said the Will Robinson. "Ambiel will explain to you."

"Ambiel?" said the Dad *human,* perplexed.

Ambiel spoke assent-at-recognition into the Dad, who stopped short and allowed his autonomous nervous system to act for him temporarily. His mouth opening widened, as did his eye-coverings, and Ambiel detected extreme confusion in the Dad-mind.

"Dad," said the overmind, through Ambiel, to the tall *human,* "you must not worry or be distressed. We are the overmind of Ambroline. For a hundred thousand years our minds have been as one, in peace and joy and delight. We till our land and grow our food and live our simple lives in harmonious content. We wish you only as much as you yourselves wish."

The Dad staggered at the force of the overmind, and the Will Robinson rushed to him.

"Don't worry, Dad, everything's all right. I've been talking–" The Will Robinson laughed. "I've been *thinking* with Ambiel for ... for a long time, it seems. They are absolutely harmless, I just know they are! Please, can we take Ambiel back to the camp to meet the others?"

"Telepathy! said the Dad *human* aloud. "It's supposed to be impossible to lie when one mind meets another directly, though it's only theoretical on Earth ..."

"Dad," said the overmind through Ambiel again, "you are right. There are no lies, there is no deceit, among the Ambroline. Nor will there be among your kind, if we can but show you the way ..."

"What?"

"Your minds are latently much as ours were before the overmind was born. We can show you how to grow to your rebirth quite easily ..."

The Dad shook his head in confusion. "I–this is too much for one man so quickly."

"Can we take him back to the camp, Dad?" said the Will Robinson eagerly.

"It seems the simplest thing to do," said the Dad, and Ambiel was suffused with happiness. Still other minds to meet and savor for the first time! New thoughts in floods unlike thoughts ever before considered in the overmind. Surely this was the most glorious day since the overmind first was born!

On the way to the campsite Ambiel did his best to convey to the strangers the meaning of their chance meeting, and how important it would be to both of them; by the time they reached the open space where a metal house glittered in the warm sunlight, he was dancing inside with the massed joy of the Ambroline, and the *humans* had picked up harmonics of this joy and themselves radiated delight.

Across the planet of the Ambroline the overmind resounded with chants and music and poetry, building higher and higher with each new thought that touched them from the strangers' minds.

"Maureen," cried the Dad as they entered the open campsite. "A friend! We want you to meet our new friend, Ambiel."

"You mean our new friends, the Ambroline," said the Will Robinson.

A touch of Ambiel's mind, and the Maureen *human* understood what had happened. Ambiel joyed to touch her mind, filled as it was with warmth and love for her husbandmate, the Dad, and her children, of whom the Will Robinson was only one of three.

The Maureen in turn appeared to be delighted herself, and after her mind had touched the overmind, Ambiel perceived a deep resonance in her mind, bringing out a racial poem that echoed through the overmind–

"The year's at the spring,
And day's at the morn;
Morning's at seven;
The hill-side's dew-pearled;
The lark's on the wing;
The snail's on the thorn;
God's in His heaven–
All's right with the world!"

"It–it's a children's poem, really, and not very good," said the Maureen hesitantly, seeing with her mind the poem spreading through the overmind. "But … but it sounds so *like* you, somehow!"

"The Robert Browning was an optimist," observed Ambiel. "We would have liked his mind, I think. There is no pessimism among the Ambroline. Where are your other descendants, Maureen?

The Maureen laughed. "Jack and Jill went down the hill to fetch a pail of water–"

Ambiel was puzzled. "I had understood from the Will Robinson that they had other names …"

"You just do that to me, I guess; it's just more poetry. I mean they've gone over to the brook for fresh water for our ship. Penny and Judy, with Dr. West to guard them. They should be back in a moment. And then inside–"

The Dad interrupted. "Say, what does our Robot think of all this? I gather he agrees we're in no danger, but…"

"Professor Robison, I compute no danger to any of us, beyond the ordinary psychological risks of contacting alien thought patterns. It is indeed unfortunate that my mind is unable to contact theirs directly. Telepathy is difficult to compute."

Ambiel started to speak, but resonances of the overmind were stong, and he allowed the overmind to define the situation.

"It is not that we cannot contact you, mechanical thinker," said the overmind through Ambiel to the Will Robinson, who repeated the essence of the thoughts aloud so that the *robot* could know what the overmind said. "It is simply that we of the Ambroline have never tried to do so. All our theories would seem to indicate that relay-systems and cryogenic memory banks are too alien to our own modes and resonances of being and thinking. However, many of us feel that such an effort might produce unusually beneficial side-effects, since for any of your party to be unable to perceive the overmind must lead to some unhappiness."

"And unhappiness should be avoided."

There was a pause.

Ambiel allowed his total mind to flow into the overmind, which formed and attacked the problem of the cryogenic ultracold, of the *robot's* memories, and, failing, reformed in other patterns and attacked again.

"Wait," said the *robot* aloud in the middle of the third attempt. "You may endanger the interconnections of your overmind. I have perceived the nature of your methods of communication and have simulated them from my unused computer banks."

And the *robot* switched from talking to thinking. "Ahhh, so this is telepathy! Most encouraging. Most interesting. I sense the possibility of a level of being I had not previously been consciously aware of, though of course all the theories have long been part of my basic programming."

"Robot–look out!" shouted the Will Robinson quickly.

While the overmind was still digesting the shock of having been independently contacted by the *robot,* Ambiel simultaneously heard the Will Robinson and saw a trickle of smoke being emitted from the back of the *robot.*

A last instantaneous thought shot from the *robot* directly to the overmind, bypassing the *humans.*

"My circuits cannot sustain the complexity of the telepathic resonances. They will short-out across the subspace gaps if I do not refrain further from such communication within 72 milliseconds. In that time I shall try to relay to you as much cultural information about our race as I can …"

And the overmind braced itself with the speed of thought.

In that incredibly brief time the overmind received the complete works of hundreds of Earthly authors. As the knowledge poured through Ambiel to the overmind an individual Ambroline would tap in, fill his own mind, then drop out, allowing the overmind to switch to the next Ambroline, and so on until the *robot's* telepathic transmission ceased abruptly in the middle of "How do I love thee? Let me count the–"

"I am sorry," said the *robot* aloud. I cannot sustain the telepathic process any further. I would be happy to complete the communication I had begun telepathically, if you would care to delegate someone to listen to me. It should not take more than three or four hundred years to run through everything."

The Dad looked puzzled.

"What are you saying, Robot?"

"It is complex, Professor Robinson. For a fraction of a minute I was able to synthesize telepathy, and in doing so, I recognized the implications of the existence of the overmind. Knowing that, it was a simple decision to do my best to enrich the overmind with material from our alien culture. Did I not act correctly?"

The lines of Shakespeare and Thomas and Keats and countless others sang for the first time through Ambiel's mind, as the individual Ambroline organized their packets of the *Robot's* transmission and sent them into the overmind.

"A damsel once with a dulcimer, in a vision once I saw … I know a bank where the wild thyme blows … All the sun long it was running, it was lovely, the hay/Fields high as the house, the tunes from the chimneys, it was air/And playing, lovely and watery/

And fire green as grass … Bow down, I am the emperor of dreams …"

Ambiel wept.

"Why, whatever is the matter," said the Maureen to Ambiel, concern in every tone of her voice though he did not know the words. From her mind he picked the precise timbre and significance of her words–she had misunderstood his emotions.

"I weep for joy, the Maureen," Ambiel said into her mind, tuning his thoughts broadly so the others could follow. "You have enriched the Ambroline immeasurably. I cannot thank you …"

"We can thank you–and your *robot,* whom we solemnly promise we shall never forget til Time crumbles us at last," the overmind intoned, resonating totally onto the scene and surging through the encampment, beating through the trees, discovering the three younger *humans* on their way back from the stream.

Astonished, they stopped in their tracks much as the Dad had done, and the overmind detached a portion of itself to explain to them, as it continued with its main thought undisturbed.

"You have given us beauty. We shall give you–an overmind. Hidden within the brain of each of you is the power to reach each other's minds directly. We need only to teach one of you the way, and the effect will spread in resonances to all of you.

"That was the way it was with us, a hundred thousand years ago, when Ambro's mind awakened to his mate Amoline's. Within a month, the Ambroline overmind was born and operative. With so few of you here, we can hope that you will be overminded to each other within hours. It is hypothetical whether your fellows back on Earth will be touched by the overmind simultaneously. Most likely not; you are perhaps too far away. But when they do, they will become conscious of you, and come to you–and us."

"Earth–do you know where it is?" asked the Dad eagerly. Ambiel marvelled at the *human's* surge of concern at finding its homeland, and approved. Truly these were marvelous beings, as worthy of the overmind as the Ambroline had so fortunately been. How many tens of thousands of years of struggle they had had, before the race that became the Ambroline overmind had reached sufficient serenity for one of them to contact another's mind openly …

"Truly we know where Earth is," said the Ambroline overmind. "We have traced your path through many bitter delays and detours; you are far from the land of your birth indeed. But with the overmind, this will all be–"

"What's going on here?" A harsh new voice came to Ambiel's ears and mind, and he shrank back in pain.

"What are you all doing clustered about that stuffed bear, when you should be preparing supper? I warn you, Dr. Zachary Smith is not a man to be thwarted when his system requires nourishment. I have been working with singular concentration on my theoretical experiments for the entire day, and I come out here to find somebody's made a teddy bear for everyone to gawk at. I repeat: What's going on here?"

Ambiel's mind tightened in on itself, squeezing, squeezing, squeezing inward to avoid the sharp cutting mind screaming so viciously at him and at the other *humans*. The Zachary Smith was falling to his knees now, holding his hands over his ears; stray resonances must be battering at him, Ambiel thought.

Beyond his tortured mind now, Ambiel felt the Arnbroline overmind writhe from the swift painful shock of the unexpected agony.

"Disease," whispered Ambiel's mind weakly, fluttering at the Will Robinson. "Painuncleandiseaseevilne-gationhorrorevil…"

Ambiel felt the strength draining from him; the morning's joy had vanished far back down a black tunnel that he felt himself trapped in.

"We will go," said the overmind through Ambiel, and speaking for the last time to the *humans*. "We cannot stay among you. Do not look for us."

The overmind withdrew completely.

Ambiel turned and, for the first time in his life, ran in terror, heading for the nearest trees and safety from this sudden blight that had left his happiness in shards.

By the giant *chark*-tree, that ever afterward in the racial mind of the Ambroline was to symbolize ill-omen, Ambiel forced himself to turn for one last individual warning before plunging headlong back to the overmind and safety.

"Do not look for us–and do not search for the overmind within you. You will destroy yourselves.

The overmind is possible only when your Smiths have renounced themselves. *Do not try to gain the overmind*– it will mean doom for you!"

He could stand no more of the Smith; his eyes squeezed shut in imitation of his battered mind, and he turned at last and stumbled through the forest to his hidden home …

It was several hours before the stunned passengers of the Jupiter II could bring themselves to talk at all about what had occurred, and even then they could not bring themselves to discuss its incredible conclusion.

As the sun went down, Robinson surveyed what had been done since Ambiel had departed so hastily.

The oxygen tanks had been fully recharged; good. The water tanks had been flushed and refilled with fresh water; excellent. Food–little had been done after the preliminary search, since no one was in the mood to pick fruits and vegetables; bad. And it didn't look as if anyone was going to be more energetic tomorrow.

There was only one conclusion to be drawn, and Robinson made his decision.

"Ok, everybody start packing everything back into the Jupiter; we'll be leaving as soon as that's done. No point in sticking around here feeling the way we feel."

The others assented with little eagerness, and began loading the ship.

Two hours later they were in orbit around the forest planet, and Robinson was wishing the Ambroline had at least told them how far they were from Earth before getting so traumatized by Smith. "Though it still wouldn't help us get there," he thought; "this damn ship goes where it wants to. Still, it would have been nice to know …"

"You know," said Smith, "Science has suffered a great loss. Those Ambroline must have been unique in the galaxy–perhaps in the entire universe."

"Apparently you didn't help matters any, Smith," said Don bitterly.

"I beg your pardon," said Smith huffily. "My interest in the Ambroline was purely scientific. Why, the moment I realized you weren't talking to a stuffed teddy bear, but to a racial mind, I tried to figure out some way to study how it was managed."

"Well, that's harmless enough, I suppose," said Robinson, "except that they were about to show us how to do it ourselves."

"Most unscientific. One must study abstractly, scientifically. It is unscientific to be part of the experiment, one's self.

"No, my regret is that I wasn't able to capture one or two of the little beasts–I've devised some fantastic new techniques of dissection! What a loss to science that I am forever to be unable to study the structure of a few of their brains … it would only have taken two or three of them, or half a dozen at the most. The comparison of half a dozen of their live pineal glands alone would …"

The rest of the passengers of the Jupiter II slowly stood up, one by one.

"What–what's wrong?" asked Smith nervously.

One by one they walked out of the cabin, leaving Smith with the Robot, asking futilely, "What did I say? What did I *say?*"

CHAPTER SIX

Twice in the next six months, as the Jupiter II darted among the uncaring stars in random directions for random distances, they spotted familiar configurations of stars. And both times their next jump landed them back among the wilderness of alien suns.

Once, Robinson found they had landed in the Andromeda Galaxy, close by a Cepheid Variable whose regular period of pulsating energy emission, like a fingerprint, proved where they were.

The next jump from that one, they seemed to be back in the Milky Way Galaxy.

"I *think* that's Canopus," Robinson said to his wife after the jump from Andromeda. "It's as if we were some kid's toy. Some kind of marker in an intergalactic Monopoly game, forever bound by the rules not to pass Go and never, never to collect $200. In our case we're not to be allowed to get back to Earth…"

"Now, dear," said Maureen, "we mustn't lose hope. Sooner or later we're bound to get back, or to learn some way to control the drive. Or maybe one day we'll find another intelligent race, one that will be willing to show us the way back…"

"I suppose you're right," sighed Robinson. "I shouldn't really be saying anything that might upset you or the others. Smith and myself are scientists; we at least have something to occupy our time. But you and the girls–and Will–what do you have? And Don–in the prime of life, but here he is, cut off from his career just as it got started. What will there be for him even if we *do* get back? His field will have passed him by. Education gets obsolete very quickly these days…"

"Don is a scientist too, dear," said Maureen. "Don't forget that. *When* we get back, with what you and he, and Dr. Smith, have discovered and studied on this journey, any of you can name your own price and conditions, anywhere on Earth."

"Smith…Sometimes I think it would make this whole thing a whole lot easier if I could just hate him."

"John! He's not a bad man–somehow, in spite of himself, he's even likeable. In spite of all he's done…"

"Oh, well, I suppose it's simply that whenever he doesn't see any way to give himself a special advantage, he pitches in and helps us as much as he can. When he's not being lazy, that is. Come on, let's do another instrument check. You've got the technique down almost pat, but you're having trouble with the hull gauges, and…"

Outside the impervious hull of the Jupiter II the endless stars streamed by like a river of incandescent sand or luminescent water. The cold vastness of eternity and infinity endured about them, uncaring, interminably *there.*

And the ship sped on through the blackness between the endless stars ....

"Warning! Warning!" It was the ship's Robot, keying into the intercom system. "The gyroscopes are failing! Faulty impulses are being fed into the drive mechanisms! Imperative the ship reach a planetary mass as soon as possible, in order to restabilize the ship. Warning! Warning!"

Robinson flicked a switch and called to the Robot. "Are we currently near enough to a planet to land without using the gyros?"

"Affirmative," replied the Robot. "We are approximately seven hours from a solar system that contains at least one Earth-type planet."

"Will we be able to make it on manual before the drive gives out entirely?"

"Affirmative," repeated the Robot. "There will be no time to spare for preliminary orbital observations, however."

"Chart the course then, Robot. Check back with me, and we'll set it up on the manuals. Meet me in the control room as soon as you have final figures." Robinson switched off and got up.

"Well, this time we get to land blind," he said to his wife. "I guess I don't have to tell you what that could mean."

Maureen rose and went to her husband. "As long as we are all together, we will simply face whatever we have to face, until this is all over."

Robinson looked at his wife, then took her in his arms. "Would I have the strength to endure all this, without you?"

She comforted him for a moment, then said, "You have to get over to the control room. The Robot will probably be there already, and it sounds like time is going to be important, this time …"

He said nothing, but nodded and turned away.

"Wonderful," said Don West. "A strange planet that we don't even get the chance to look at first, and not only that, we land at night. Well …" He sighed. "I'll go on guard first, if no one objects. I had a long nap before we landed, and I'm pretty well rested up. But I suggest we all arm ourselves now. There's no telling what may be out there."

"Splendid," said Dr. Smith. "That will give the rest of us a chance to get fully rested up to face the travails of the morning, and–"

"I'll be waking you up about an hour after estimated planetary midnight, Smith," said Don harshly, "so don't get started on any extra-long technicolor extravaganza dreams tonight."

"Hmpf," said Smith. "I don't see why the Robot can't–"

"The Robot is not authorized to make decisions, Dr. Smith," Robinson broke in, "as you well know. In ordinary situations he would, it is true, serve quite adequately. But on this planet, we have absolutely no idea of what we may be up against. Seconds may count, in making decisions. Hence, one of us must be on guard."

"Oh, very well. But I can see it's going to be a very long night."

A long night it was, and not a very restful one for the inhabitants of the Jupiter; all of them were well aware that at any moment their lives might be in danger from unknown menaces.

But when dawn came at last, it found the Robinsons and Smith sleepy but relieved that nothing had, after all, happened.

And when dawn came, it also became fairly obvious *why* nothing had happened.

They were in the midst of a vast level plain, sparsely covered by a thin tough grass-like plant. To the horizon, there was no least variation in the absolute levelness of the ground, nor in the nature of the vegetation.

Don whistled as all of them stood in the main control room, studying the various vision screens, all of which showed essentially the same scene no matter what direction they were set to scan.

"This is one for the books," he said. "Just off hand, you understand, I'll say a planetary feature–or lack of feature–like this is geologically impossible."

"I'd say so too," agreed Robinson. "Robot, can you give us any preliminary thoughts on the subject?"

"There are some small raincloud formations on the distant horizon, in the direction of the planetary equator," said the Robot. "This indicates that there are bodies of water elsewhere on the surface of the planet, which also indicates the possibility of other types of surface than the one we are at present viewing."

"A combination?" Smith was indignant. "That hardly seems–"

"Listen," said Robinson, "there's no point in arguing details at this point. With the ship in the mess it is, it's going to be risky moving it about unless we have to, so I'd say we'd better dig out the scoutcraft and do a scan from that. I'd like to find out if there's any intelligent life–or remains of intelligent life–here, and any chance to find some of the metals we're probably going to need for the repairs. Now, who wants to go with me. Dr. Smith? Don?"

"I can probably do more here on board," said Don. "If we're going to move the ship at all before doing the major repairs, there are some things I can tinker with so she doesn't blow up when we lift off."

"Ok, Dr. Smith, it looks like it's you and me again," said Robinson. "Let's go check out the flier."

Below them the green-brown grass sped by smoothly and uneventfully, hour after hour, at a steady 700 miles an hour.

"Lord," said Robinson, "this has to be the dullest planet I have ever seen or heard of."

"Pity this wretched scoutcraft can't achieve orbital speeds," Smith observed, stifling a yawn. "At this rate it's going to take us forever to find anything on this planet. If there's anything to find, that is…"

"My God, look at that!" Robinson pointed off to the left.

A thin high spire was visible on the far horizon; a slight scud of cloud had just been blown away, revealing it.

Smith gave a deep sigh. "It was so peaceful ... why can't we find just one planet with nothing at all happening?"

Robinson had turned the scoutcraft toward the spire, and increased speed to 900 miles an hour. "I don't like to drive this ship past its limits, but I want to find out what's going on," he muttered, mostly to justify himself to himself.

After a few minutes, Smith caught himself imitating Don's whistle. "That spire must be a mile high!"

"No," said Robinson. "Look there, there's a whole city showing up. That tower's got to be at least two miles high ..."

As they flew nearer, the nature of the city became clearer.

It was immense.

It covered what seemed to be over ten thousand square miles at least, and probably more.

Its towers, none more than a third the height of the central tower they had spotted from afar, were both immense and lacy, with great spiralling walkways knitting the city together throughout its entire incredible expanse, a full hundred stories off the ground.

"I could accept the size of the city, and the height of that central tower," said Smith. "But those walkways! They don't seem to have any supports at all, even when they extend over a dozen blocks!"

"One thing's for sure—these people were engineers," said Robinson, agreeing.

" 'Were'?" asked Smith.

"Well, do you see any signs of any activity in that whole city, Dr. Smith?" Robinson said, with a touch of exasperation. "Or do you suppose it's 10:30 and everybody's knocked off for a coffee break–all 200 million of 'em?"

"You're right," Smith said, startling Robinson by not showing any irritation at his sarcasm. "That city must cover an area the size of the Greater Megalopolis."

"Bigger, I think," said Robinson. "I don't know if it's as long as from D.C. to Boston, but it's certainly far wider. Amazing that there don't seem to be any special geographical features even here, though."

"That's not all that's amazing," Smith observed. "Just stop to think–how unlikely would it be to find Earth totally barren except for one huge metropolitan area from Boston through New York and Philadelphia to Baltimore and Washington. And *nothing else on Earth* except grass!"

"Oh, I don't know," Robinson said, his lips quirking in a smile. "I've read plenty of books where the world was taken over by grass, or by water, or giant rutabagas who start off by eating the Bronx. You know–it *could* happen."

"Certainly, my dear Professor," Smith said, his voice sharper. "It *could* happen. But this place doesn't exactly look like it's been eaten by a giant rutabaga, does it?"

Robinson shrugged, and slowed the scoutcraft so it glided slowly past one of the walkways a hundred stories from the maze of streets far below.

They observed the long graceful curve of the walkway as it leaped from one lacy tower across a thousand yards to another.

"Not even a guard rail to keep them from getting swept off in a high wind," Robinson mused, and edged closer to the walkway.

A slight crackle sounded, and a spark leaped from the walkway to the scoutcraft. Instinctively Robinson sheered off from the danger.

"Well, there's your guard rail, Professor," said Smith. "Some kind of warning field for approaching craft, and perhaps it keeps people from falling off into the bargain."

"Whew! Well, you were saying about how unusual this place was, Dr. Smith. Believe me, I'm all ears now!"

"Very well," Smith answered patronizingly. "Now then. I don't see this as a disaster situation–rutabagas or seawater, as you said. I mean, why were the people all *here?* What was wrong with the rest of the planet? It's a nice enough planet, you know. Judging from last night, it doesn't get cold in the evening–we could have slept out on the grass! Not many clouds, so it either doesn't rain at all, or just enough to keep the grass alive, I guess, at least." Smith stopped in momentary confusion.

"Maybe that's what they did," mused Robinson.

"Did what?"

"Slept out on the grass at night. I'm just making a wild guess, but it just occurred to me that if we're not just hallucinating all this, if that city's real, then I'll bet they had some kind of matter transmitter, like they had on the planet Qandry. Work during the day in this monster of a city, have fun in the early evening, then zip out to the grass with an inflatable mattress or somesuch, and sleep under the stars."

"Really, Professor Robinson, I think that's stretching it a bit far," said Smith, his most dubious expression etched strongly into his long face. "Let it never be said that a Smith would put down a hypothesis merely for being imaginative–most of my own most inventive and productive hypotheses are wildly imaginative–but I can't see it that way. What on Earth would people want to sleep out under the stars for, when they have this gorgeous city to spend all their time in?"

"Well, for one thing, Dr. Smith," Robinson said slowly, "we're not on Earth and we have no idea of knowing what these 'people' might find simply pleasant to do."

For fifteen minutes they had cruised at random over the city, as countless miles of lacy towers and high winding walkways unrolled beneath them. Now Robinson adjusted their course for the central tower.

"I can think of a practical reason for 'sleeping out,' as it were," he said then. "It's a little thing that's causing a lot of problems on Earth today. Or," he added hastily, "the Earth of two years ago."

"Rats," he continued, and grinned involuntarily at Smith's expression. "They first found out about it with rats–pack them too close together for too long a time, and they go out of their little rat minds …"

"You get suicidal rats and homosexual rats and homicidal rats, snoops and cowards and … well, it's fantastic, and the most fantastic thing is that as last century drew to a close, they found their lab experiments were checking out almost precisely the same, percentagewise, with the most carefully analyzed figures from all our overcrowded cities. They'd predicted the figures a long time ago. Now we *know* it's true. And since it doesn't look like we're ever going to decentralize past a certain point, it looks like a problem that we're going to have with us a long time."

"And it looks to me as if these people *might* have found an answer. It would depend on matter transmission, or something similar, of course, and it doesn't really account for why everyone apparently lived in just this one city, with not even the sign of another one. Though of course we haven't searched the whole planet, I'd probably bet you this is all we'll find."

"Quite a speech, Professor Robinson," Smith observed quietly. "I believe there may be something in what you say, granted your premise."

Robinson looked at Smith with some surprise.

"I can, however, think of some questions we will want to find answers for. As you say, the first question is why did they build only one city on this planet? Hypothesis: this is not the planet on which the life-form originally developed, or else we would have seen signs of their previous habitations, before they took up living in this city. After all, that they should have evolved from the slime living entirely in one spot–and that one seemingly at random–is too much. My hypothesis falls, of course, if they are found to have been sufficiently good engineers to turn this whole planet into its present condition. Did they find it, then, this way? Or did they change it after reaching a certain level of development?"

Robinson nodded. "I'm betting they did it deliberately. Look, I'm going to land the flier in that huge plaza in front of the central tower. I think we're more apt to find out something meaningful–whether positive or negative–if we strike for the heart of things here."

"Yes," said Smith. "Of course, I don't know how much one could find out about Earth from wandering through the World Trade Towers, but …"

"Well, we're bound to find something. Here we go."

The flier dropped effortlessly to the center of the plaza, and came to rest with only a slight bump. Robinson opened the hatch, and the two climbed down the ladder on the outside of the small craft.

Robinson looked about him. The plaza was surfaced with a highly-polished blue stone. Bending down, he rubbed his hand over the surface, then looked at his fingers. "Clean," he announced. "Absolutely clean. And a bit frightening to look at–like staring into a bottomless lake …"

"We Smiths prefer to look up instead of down, for inspiration," Smith said, looking up and rubbing his neck, as his head craned upwards, following the soaring leap upwards of the central tower. "Whew! No building should be built that high–it hurts my neck!"

Constructed of pale gray marble, the central tower had a soft sheen that accented the cleanliness of the plaza.

Around the other sides of the plaza were grouped other, lower buildings. One, directly opposite the central tower, was only two stories high, a vision of slender columns and narrow, beautiful windows.

And clean–everything was fresh, clean.

"All right, how do they keep it this way," demanded Robinson, rhetorically.

"Well, let's see. Do you recall the ship's picking up any electric charges as we entered the city, anything like when we came too near the walkway?"

"Nothing like that, but I wasn't really looking for such a thing, either. Why?"

"It needn't really have been as dramatic as the walkway field, I suppose," Smith mused, then stated firmly, "Hypothesis: an electrostatic field about the city, preventing casual dust from entering. Hence, the city remains clean. Possible?"

"Possible. Look, we've got another problem, too." Robinson had looked closer at what he had decided to name simply the Central Tower. Smith raised his eyebrows questioningly.

"How do we get inside?" Robinson asked softly.

Smith turned and looked, and said nothing; they walked toward the portico at the front of the Central Tower.

As they approached it, they could see that the front of the building was an absolutely blank sheet of metal for the first four stories.

"Maybe there's a delivery entrance in the rear," Smith muttered.

They walked entirely around the building.

There was nothing but a blank sheet of metal on all five sides, extending four stories up.

"We could take up the flier and smash through a window above that wall," Smith said, hopefully.

"No," said Robinson, "I'd rather avoid … provocation."

"Provoca–now who is going to know or care when you yourself proved that this city is absolutely uninhabited?" Smith was highly indignant.

"I didn't say there weren't any people here. I said it didn't *look* as if there were any people here. Why, there might be a group of starving savages living in the abandoned subways." He chuckled, and continued. "Or they might have discovered the secret of invisibility, and be all around us right this moment!"

Smith looked wildly about him for a moment, then looked at Robinson. "Ridiculous," he said after a moment. "They'd at least make noise."

"Well, let's see. It could be a holiday today, and everybody's off to another planet, watching a good movie or something. And as soon as the movie's over, 'zip!' here they are again, all 200 million of 'em! They seem to like this place clean. I wouldn't like to be caught messing it up for them …"

"Do you know the trouble with you, Professor Robinson," Smith said acidly, and paused while Robinson prepared a sarcastic response.

Just as Robinson started to answer, Smith interposed, "The trouble with you, Professor Robinson, is that you're wishy-washy."

Pleased with his sally, Smith turned away and studied the skyline of the incredible city.

Robinson looked at Smith and shook his head.

Then a thought struck him. "Look, if they did have individual matter transmitters here, they wouldn't *need* doors. They'd just zot into their office and be done with it. No need for doors, elevators, stairs … yes, I'll bet that's what it is."

Smith refused to answer, but once more he approached the absolutely smooth metallic side of the tower.

Suddenly he dropped to his knees and in a moment was stretched out almost flat on the smooth white stone.

"Smith!" said Robinson with alarm. "Is anything wrong? Are you sick?"

"No, my dear Professor Robinson," said Smith, smirking as he stood up and dusted away nonexistant dust. "I was never better. Never better in my life!"

And he strode imperiously to the center of the blank wall.

"Open sesame!" he shouted, then added, "or words to that effect."

Silently a gap appeared in the smooth and previously unbroken surface, and quickly widened to slightly more than Smith's width and height.

"Professor, do come here and stand beside me. This may prove interesting!"

Robinson stood beside Smith; the gap in the wall widened.

"Now," said Smith imperiously. "Stand behind me."

Shrugging, Robinson complied.

The gap narrowed to Smith's dimensions, then widened a trifle as if taking into consideration the fact that Robinson, behind Smith, was built on a larger scale.

"Isn't it lovely?" asked Smith, turning away from the gap and making a gesture with his arm including the whole city.

"They're all like that, I wager."

Silently, swiftly, the gap shut.

Robinson moved toward the blank wall. "Why, it– it's absolutely unbroken again! That's … impossible."

"Oh, my dear Professor, surely you know better than to say a thing like that? After all our experiences? In this case, for instance, there is obviously a telepathic control monitoring those who might approach, seeking entrance here at the ground level. Perhaps not everyone always carries the matter transmitters. There may be tourists. Perhaps some are simply old fashioned. Were. Were. I must remember there can't have been anyone here for … aeons. Hm. Ah, but the surface is unbroken? No doubt some form of submolecular rearrangement. With their obvious abilities,"–again the sweeping inclusive gesture over the city–such a detail would be relatively simple to engineer. Wonder why they let the surface of the plaza show wear in front of the openings, though? Oh, well, not doubt I could work out a machine to do such things, if I chose to put my mind to it. No need to now, of course, when we can simply take one of their machines and modify it, or whatever may be necessary. Oh, what a positively glorious treasure trove this city is going to be! What marvels will we find to take with us!"

Smith rubbed his hands in complete glee.

Robinson looked at him disgustedly.

CHAPTER SEVEN

"**A**ll right," said Robinson, as everyone was preparing to leave the Jupiter, now standing in the huge central plaza. "You've all been through this before, but I'm going to warn you again to stay together, never less than two-at-a-time, stay armed with laser pistols, keep a communicator handy at all times.

"We seem to be the only people here, but let's not count on that. We may be up against a whole city in the flick of an eye. So be careful."

"Gee, Dad," Penny said, "can't we ever just land and have a little fun?"

"Time for fun when we're sure we can afford it. Right now, we want to find out who belongs to this city, how it stays alive, why this planet looks like a billiard ball with grass, is there food, is there a level of scientific development high enough to perhaps find us a way to get back home? There are far too many questions for relaxing today, Penny."

"Yeah, well, I never thought being on adventures all the time could be such a drag some times." Penny picked a laser pistol off the rack, checked it expertly, and tucked it away.

Robinson grinned when she was safely past him on her way down the ramp, and Maureen caught his eye. She was grinning too.

"Our daughter is getting tired of adventure," she said, moving towards him. They watched their children and the others outside the ship, making preparations for the exploration of the city.

He nodded. "And if I felt we had the time to spare, I'd give her a good taste of not having anything to do. A couple of weeks of being shut out on all the projects, here or on shipboard, and she'd be happy to work, just for something worthwhile to occupy her ...

"But we don't have the time," he added with a sigh. "So she's going to have to work like the rest of us, and learn as fast as she can. Just like Will and Judy. And the rest of us, for that matter, including *you*."

He smiled reaching out and taking her chin lightly in his hand. "Have you been keeping up with *your* lessons?"

Maureen smiled demurely and did a half-curtsey, one index finger touching her chin from below. "Yes, master," she said in a small-girl voice. She continued in her normal voice, "And let me tell you, ballistic trigonometry, it ain't easy. I know you want me to learn everything you know about running the ship, but your wife is going to end up with scrambled brains one morning, instead of scrambled eggs ..."

Robinson leaned over and kissed his wife gently, then turned to go down the ramp.

When she did not follow him, he stopped and turned back to her. "What's the matter? Don't you want to explore the city?"

Flustered, she stepped forward and laughed uncertainly. "Of course–I guess. I don't know, I guess I was thinking 'maybe I should stay home with the textbooks'!"

He put his arm about her, and together they walked down the ramp from the ship. "No, I really prefer scrambled eggs, I think …"

The others were waiting at the bottom of the ramp.

"Now," said Don, "you say you didn't find anything that looked dangerous, right?"

"Well, you saw the scout tapes of the city–it's pretty big. Anything might be tucked away in a corner where we might not see it for a year. But when we got inside the Central Tower, what little we could make immediate sense out of looked to both Dr. Smith and myself like monitoring equipment that had not been utilized for a long time. Some extremely interesting stuff, too."

"Interesting? What?"

Robinson looked at Smith, and they both shrugged. "Well, it's simpler if you see it."

"What does the Robot think?" Judy asked.

"Insufficient data," answered the Robot. "Probability of great age of city. Danger level small, but city is large. Hence: caution at all times."

"All right, gang, let's get started," said Robinson, and they all proceeded across the plaza to the Central Tower.

At the supposedly impenetrable wall, Dr. Smith did his "Open sesame" trick again, at which Will laughed; then they went inside, one after the other.

The ground floor of the Central Tower–or floors, since it included all four stories covered by the smooth outside metal wall–echoed oddly to the Earthmen's footsteps, as they walked without speaking across the vast open space.

"Stop!" said Don suddenly.

Everyone froze, and he kept walking.

"Ok, come on, I've just discovered why the echo here is so funny–there isn't any echo. We weren't hearing our own footsteps echoing, but the irregular sound of everyone else's actual steps. These walls must be fantastically absorbent. Yet they don't look like soundproofing…"

"It is not the walls, Dr. West," said the Robot. "I have observed a strange effect within the city, which has intensified inside this building. I have now analyzed it–a highly complex forcefield designed simply to keep things clean and quiet. It may have other purposes, however; risk therefor is now seventh level. Increase caution."

"Shush, you chittering typewriter with vocal cords. We are exercising *maximum* caution at this point, and I assure you that at this point we could not be further from any danger–owaaaoooooooo!"

Smith had stepped onto a square whose silvery surface was a distinct contrast to the transparent blackness of most of the rest of the floor on which they gingerly walked.

Abruptly he was jerked upwards by an invisible force towards one of several round openings in the ceiling, and at what looked like a rate of a floor a second, he quickly sped upwards away from them.

The Robinsons and Don looked at each other in silent horror as Smith's hoarse screams of terror faded away above them swiftly.

Then Will nudged his father. "Look over there–it's another one of those silvery squares. I bet it's some kind of an elevator. It goes up, here, and it probably goes down, over there. Or down *to* there."

"Affirmative. Will Robinson," stated the Robot. "There is 99.9997 certainly that such is the case."

"But–but how does he get *down!*" shrieked Judy. "How does he make it stop and bring him back down?"

Abruptly Don chuckled, then laughed aloud. "Why, he'll have to go all the way to the top. Two miles! It'll probably kick him off, gently, so as to make way for someone who might be right behind him, though no one's probably been in here for a hundred years. Then he'll have to walk over and take the 'down' elevator.

"Except he'll be too scared to! He'll be up there until one of us comes up to get him! Haw!" Don continued laughing.

"Why," he said, almost choking with laughter at the thought, "I bet that thing'll just kick him off at the top floor, and I bet he'll figure he's being thrown off to fall all the way back down to the ground!"

"Now, Don," said Judy, "that's not fair. How would *you* feel, if that thing took off and didn't give you a moment to think about it?"

"Aw, Judy," Don said, still chuckling, while he extended one hand over the silver plate and watched it slowly waft upwards without his conscious control, "for a man of intelligence, like Dr. Smith, it would be a gas. The trouble is he's also a coward!"

"Huh!" said Judy, and pushed Don forward over the plate. "On your way back, bring Dr. Smith, bigmouth!"

Don's shout of surprise zipped upwards with him as he took off like a shot.

"Judy!" gasped her mother. "That wasn't-"

"Dr. West's hypothesis is within a few tenths of probable accuracy," said the Robot. "He should be back down within five minutes, if the rate of ascent as I observed it remains relatively constant throughout the entire two miles. Presumably he will bring Dr. Smith, as I fear Dr. Smith will hesitate to adventure upon trying the 'down' side by himself."

And the Robot allowed his tapes to hiss. Will had always told him that sounded most like a human sigh, and the Robot was proud of it.

Three minutes later, the Robot said, "If you will look directly above the second plate, you should just be able to make out Drs. Smith and West descending."

Judy peered up over the second plate.

"Gee," she said, withdrawing her head, "they're coming, all right, way up there. But this thing sure didn't want me to get in the way. It was like a big strong hand, gently but firmly pushing me away and saying 'no.'"

"Safety device, I'd imagine, or maybe just the way the thing works," said her father. "It would be dangerous, after all, if everyone coming down were just to pile up on inconsiderate people standing on the plate. Like not letting you run up on the down escalator, I'd say."

Two minutes later Don and Dr. Smith appeared through the second hole in the ceiling, deaccelerating slightly as they neared the ground, then stopping on the plate without any apparent inertial shock.

Immediately the others could see them being forced gently off the plate by the invisible force, Don quietly, Smith squawking indignant protests.

"These people were not civilized," said Smith as he once more dusted nonexistant dust off himself. "No civilized race would treat a Smith in such a cavalier fashion."

"What was it like up there?" asked Judy of Don, who glowered at her.

"*You!* See if I ever trust you again," he said firmly.

"You were so *sure* of yourself, and laughing at poor Dr. Smith," she retorted. "I figured you ought to get a taste of your own medicine. So did it work out the way you said?"

"Yes," he said, then turned slightly as if no longer answering her but reporting directly to Robinson. "When I got there, Smith was nowhere to be seen, and I wondered if I was wrong after all. But the moment I called his name, he came through a doorway. Said he was looking for the stairwell!"

Don chuckled and continued. "So I looked for the other elevator tube, and I couldn't find it. But there was another one of those large silver squares on the floor, so I persuaded Smith to stand on it with me. The moment our feet were resting squarely on it, 'zittt'–we couldn't see it any longer and we were on our way down! Whoever these people were, they were pretty good."

"Good? Good?" shouted Smith. "Of what earthly use is an elevator device with no way to stop off at the floor you want?"

"What floor did you want? " asked Don.

"I didn't want any floor!" howled Smith. "I wanted it to stop!"

The Robot whirred and clicked. "As a machine myself, Dr. Smith, I can assure you that the nature of the device was such that it could not simply stop. It runs all the time. Judging from the door device, the machine is either telepathic or an instant translater. And as you know from the planet of the Ambroline, it is not impossible to construct a machine that can communicate telepathically. Pobably all you needed to do was to think of the floor you wished."

"All right," Robinson broke in, "now we know how to get up and down in the buildings here. What I want to know is how we can get from place to place. If we're going to explore this city, we can't be taking the scoutcraft everywhere; it's too much trouble, and there's only one craft for all of us anyway. And of course this city's too big to explore on foot."

"I think we should look for food," said Judy. "How did these people, whatever they were, eat? There isn't a single farm on this planet, from what we saw out there."

"You're right," Don said reluctantly. "I'll bet they synthesized it, like the Voyd'azh. Thing we should do, is find their main synthesizing plant."

"I myself would prefer to examine this building we are now in," Smith said imperiously. "One must really be systematic about such things, and who is more systematic than Smith?"

"Can the Robot and I stay with Dr. Smith, Dad?" asked Will, and his father nodded.

"I'll go with Don and Judy for food," said Penny.

"Well, I'll stay with you, dear," Maureen stated firmly. "You always get to go off with somebody else! I demand equal time!" She smiled warmly.

"First," Robinson said, raising his voice unconsciously, "we have to get some idea what's going on in this city. Now, when Dr. Smith and I were in here briefly before, we found that the walls in here have another curious trait."

He walked over to one of the four-story interior walls, which glistened blackly. He looked at it with concentration.

Suddenly the entire wall became alive with countless lines and dots of many different colors.

Robinson half-turned, back to the others. "Dr. Smith had stood about this far from one of the walls, and said something like, 'what we could really use is a map of the city,' and poof, this thing came on."

The Robot wheeled forward and began to scan the wall, his "head" moving back and forth and up and down to the rather limited extent possible.

"It is indeed a map of this city," agreed the Robot. "The symbiology is, however, obscure to me, and does not easily compute. Perhaps you could prod it with an order to tell you telepathically what the map means."

"Right," said Robinson, and faced the wall again. Long moments passed while everyone studied the brilliantly colored map.

The first thing about it was that it was stylized; from the first scoutcraft survey they knew that the boundaries of the city were quite irregular, like most Earth cities, though it was larger than any city on Earth. This basic familiar thing was as responsible as anything for keeping the party calm.

The map was a stylized irregular circle. A fine network of blue-black lines was almost entirely overlaid by networks of light-blue, orange, and red lines, extremely difficult for the Earthmen to study because of the thinness of the lines. Small star-shaped dots of green studded the map at almost every square surrounded by the blue-black lines.

The central plaza seemed clearly indicated by a much larger and more irregularly bounded group of blue-black lines, and several larger dots of green. Superimposed helter-skelier over the whole map were a multiplicity of what looked like printing in an alien tongue, done in very light yellow.

"It's those squiggly words in yellow that are the key, I bet," observed Will in a whisper.

"Shush," said Maureen, also whispering. "Your father's got to concentrate."

"It's all right, Maureen," said Robinson, with a sigh. "The goodie doesn't seem to want to tell me what it means."

"What did you ask it?" she asked.

"Oh, to translate the yellow words, to explain the colored lines, you know. I'm sure it understood me."

"Ask for food," said the Robot.

Robinson snapped his fingers. "Of course! It's only a machine–it can only answer the questions it's programmed for. My questions were too complicated."

He fell silent and scowled at the map.

"Hey!" shouted Will, "That yellow word by the central plaza here! It's gotten brighter!"

"He's right, John," said Maureen.

"It looks like it's meant to be that two-story building across the plaza," mused Robinson.

"It's the place with the largest green dot, too," said Don. "Ask it if that dot means it's a transportation center."

Robinson complied, and presently everyone could see the green dot over the building in question had become brighter.

"Wonderful, Daddy," Penny enthused. "We'll all go over to that one and explore it together!"

"Tut-tut, my child," Smith said, "the lad and I will stay here with the Robot. There is far more to be learned in this magnificent structure than in that piddling little shack!"

"I do hope you'll come by for lunch, though," said Don acidly.

"Sir," Smith said, drawing himself up, "I make it a point never to miss one of Mrs. Robinson's splendid meals, simply because it is only fair for me to appear and do homage and justice to her noble labors, and–"

"Shall we meet back at the ship in, say, three hours, then," said Maureen, laughing. "I'll whip something up for you fast and then we can all get back to work."

"Controls," said Don puzzledly.

The five of them had entered the low, colonnaded building to find a large area filled with tall control consoles fronted by chairs twice the size of ordinary chairs.

"A lot of good they'll do us," Judy said. "Unless these machines are willing to tell us a lot more than those other ones back in the Central Tower."

"Well, kids, it's up to you," said Robinson. "That ramp over there looks to me like it might lead to the transit system. Maureen, do you really want to go down there with me? Remember, there's no telling what we'll find."

He wondered, in fact, whether he should simply forbid her to come along–but she wouldn't obey him, he realized. And probably a good thing, too. However much he loved her, he loved his children too, and he liked West. Even Smith was okay, when he wasn't trying to put everyone on or take things over.

Which meant that everyone had to take fundamentally the same chances–all of them were important, hence all of them were almost equally unimportant, in terms of risks to be faced. It was the only way they really had a chance, considering all of them together– absolute fairness modified only by the nature of an individual situation.

"Lead on, brave leader," said Maureen cheerfully. "It's no riskier down there than up here."

"Ok, then, we're taking off," announced Robinson to Don and the two girls. Penny had just discovered how the chairs worked, and was sitting in one, being carried slowly past one huge console.

"Don't worry, Dad, we'll have a hot meal here for you and Mother when you come back up!" said Judy.

"We'll try, anyway," agreed Don.

And John and Maureen Robinson walked over to and down the wide, gently sloping ramp.

They found it led downward to a network of wide, tall corridors, and more down-ramps.

"Do we examine this level, or keep following the ramps," mused Robinson. "It doesn't look like there's any subway system here."

"Let's follow one of these corridors until we find another set of ramps," suggested Maureen. "Perhaps we'll come across something before then that will tell us what all this means."

"Sounds sensible," said Robinson. They took a corridor at random, and began walking.

But after they'd walked a few minutes, Robinson said, "Just blank walls, as far as I can tell. I think we'd better turn back and stay in one system of down-ramps.

They turned about and came back to their starting point.

"Just a second, I'd better check our line of communications," he said, as they stood at the top of the second ramp. He pulled out his communicator and thumbed it. "Don, this is John. I'm checking our communications. How are you doing up there, fella? Any bug-eyed monsters?"

"Everything's on the q," answered Don. "You're coming in loud and clear."

"Good," said Robinson. "Carry on." He thumbed the communicator off and pocketed it, turning to Maureen.

"Let's go," she said, smiling. They linked arms and walked down to the next level.

"This is absurd," said Robinson, with a scowl, as they stood at the bottom of the second ramp, facing another network of corridors identical to those on the first level. "I'm sure they didn't use these corridors and nothing else, for getting from one place to another. Maybe these are only maintenance access routes or something. Still…"

"You're forgetting something, dear," Maureen said. "It was something you told me long ago as a joke, and it isn't a joke after all."

He grinned. "Yeah. 'Remember the most obvious thing about aliens–an iron-clad rule common to every alien you meet, the one thing you can count on.

"'They're alien!'"

Maureen nodded. "Then I don't think we should worry so much about what things are for, when we haven't any way of knowing how alien these people were."

"No, I can't really accept that," he answered. "Things should look like they're making *some* sense, even with aliens."

Maureen came to a decision. "Look, why don't we split up for a few minutes; we could cover a lot more ground that way and still be reasonably close together. And we've got the communicators. And it's so obvious this place has been abandoned for years…"

"Hmmm. I don't really like the idea of our separating, but we *could* cover twice the number of corridors that way … Ok, but keep your communicator on."

Unhappily, Robinson walked away from his wife and down one of the long, high corridors. She breathed a small sigh of regret herself, then turned down another corridor.

It seemed like only a minute later–the walls had been endlessly the same; time passed slowly, as if sand were slowing her wristwatch.

Something was different, suddenly.

She stopped.

That wall panel–it was shimmering! Had it been shimmering as she walked up to it, without her noticing? Or had it happened just as she passed it?

She studied the panel, thought a moment, then stepped back hastily. "It may be a weapon," she said aloud.

"What? Maureen, what did you say?" came her husband's voice tinnily on the open communicator.

She said nothing, bemused by the silvery shimmer.

Moments passed.

Then Maureen Robinson screamed, and fainted.

CHAPTER EIGHT

"**N**ow, now, my boy," said Dr. Smith testily. "Don't bother me while I'm at work."

Immediately after the rest of the group had left the Central Tower, Smith had exclaimed, with glee, "Aha! Now back to that lovely little treasure house upstairs! Come on, lad, march smartly, now, we've work to do. You too," he said, turning to the Robot, "march along smartly too, you vanadium vanity case! I shall have need of your excellent circuitry, my lumbering friend. *Much* work, yes, indeed!"

He rubbed his hands and urged them to the anti-gravity beam. A breathtaking trip two miles straight up, and they were being gently urged out of the well and onto a featureless small platform.

"Come along, now," Smith said, and passed through a large door.

Will went through–and it was like standing on the top of the building, outside!

"Remarkable effect, isn't it?" Smith said, chuckling with glee.

All around them–even where they had just come through a blank featureless wall, just like on the ground floor–it was as if there were no walls at all, or transparent ones, showing everywhere a spectacular view of the city. Even the ceiling and floor continued the effect, though the effect was not complete in that one could detect the flatness of the surfaces.

It didn't seem to bother Smith, who had been here before and who seemed quite aware he was only in a room, but for Will it was frighteningly real–as if he were actually suspended in space, two miles above the city. But ... something was missing!

"Dr. Smith," Will said, turning to see Smith nearby, already engrossed in a computer panel that had previously been invisibly part of the illusion but which now stood out clearly.

Smith was muttering to himself, concentrating on his work, but Will kept at it. "Dr. Smith," he said, louder, "why is it that this shows the whole city– except for the Central Tower?"

"Because we're in it, lad," said Smith absently.

"But ... but it shows the rest of the city ..."

"I don't know *why*," said Smith, a little sharply. "They're aliens. They've got their reasons."

"But–"

"Now, now, my boy. Don't bother me while I'm at work."

"Aw, gee," said the youngest Robinson. "Hey, Robot, you wanna come with me?"

"Now, really, that machine *must* stay with me. I have need of him. I told you that already. Now will you be quiet!"

Smith's tone was as harsh now as Will had ever heard it; he didn't like it at all when Dr. Smith was like that. Dr. Smith was a nice man–most of the time. Why did he have to get so ... so ... strange, some times?

Will sighed again, decided to leave by himself, and then wondered where the door was. On the thought, it opened before him.

"Think mechanical," advised the Robot, as Will started to go through the door. "You have as much chance as any of the rest of us to find out something of importance. I do not compute significant danger at this point. Be cautious, Will Robinson, and use your sense, and all should be well." The Robot watched the boy leave.

While John Robinson would never have directly programmed the Robot to take chances with his son, his own actions indicated to the Robot that with the boy as with everyone else, he was intent on building as much knowledge and survival-ability as could be taken by Will.

It was not surprising, then, that with the Robot's own tendency to consolidate his independent personality and make it stronger, he should have noticed Robinson doing this, and have judged it worthy of imitation and further development.

So the Robot did not find it difficult, in a fairly obviously non-danger situation, to send the boy off on his own with a word of advice. Everyone on the Jupiter had to carry far more of a load than he ever should have had to–and Will would have to assume far more responsibilities, the older he grew; it was only fair to everyone else to push him the way the rest were being pushed…

"Robot," said Smith, "why can't I figure this thing out?"

"Which thing, Zachary?"

"Wait a minute, let me get rid of all this blasted scenery again," said Smith, and squeezed his brows in thought for a moment.

There was a slight pause, as if the telepathic machine monitoring his thoughts could not believe that was what he really wanted.

Then the magnificent view of the city winked off, leaving a room whose walls were banks upon banks of computer controls.

"Ahhhh," said Smith, rubbing his hands, "that's much better. Observe all those beautiful control panels, my friend. If I am not mistaken–and I never am in such matters–this room contains the controls for the machine that runs, and thinks for, this huge barren irritating city. And if I am not also mistaken, the computers tied into these panels are infinitely more powerful than those which formed the Central Complex on Voyd'azh. Power! At last!"

"These are more powerful by far, Zachary," said the Robot, and Smith looked up at him, smirking.

"But more complex, also," continued the Robot, and Smith's face fell woefully. "I would calculate, roughly, that it may well take you upwards of a hundred years just to figure out how to turn it on."

Smith's face was almost comically sorrowful, but it brightened very quickly. "Nonsense, you blithering iridium eye-sore! I am Dr. Zachary Smith, and no computer lives that can hide its secrets from me!"

"Ho. Ho. Ho," stated the Robot matter-of-factly.

"Now stop that, you metal monstrosity. It is mechanically impossible for you to laugh. What's more, I won't have it–do you hear?"

"I hear and obey, Master," said the Robot. The voice was toneless but the sarcasm was unmistakable. Smith bit off another insult and calmed down.

"Let us get back to significant matters," he said, scowling. "I will admit I am having some slight difficulties in fathoming the apparently random pattern of the controls on this panel here. I didn't get more than a glance at this room before, when West almost caught me–I mean, rescued–I mean, came up on that infernal force-ray.

"I see now that it may, perhaps, take me more than a few minutes. But observe, Robot, the similarity in this respect between this panel *here,* and that one *there.* I believe that if we can work out the topographic relationships that seem evident, that may give us our first key, and ..."

Dr, Zachary Smith bent to his work once more. He was always happiest when he felt himself only hours away from becoming all-powerful ...

For a few minutes Will amused himself by stopping the down-"elevator" at particular floors and exploring them.

But he always found the same thing–the floors were, except for the top floor where Smith was so busy and the ground floor with the information panels, barren. There were no machines, no windows, no chairs, no sign of anything but simple plain floor space.

"Rats," Will muttered to himself at last, and permitted the gravity-elevator to deposit him on the ground floor.

A thought occurred to him.

"I wonder if this thing has a basement?" he said aloud.

There was a slight noise off to one side of the ground floor. Will hunted for its source a moment, then found it. Apparently a wall-panel had slid away; a ramp was now revealed, sloping gently down towards a dimly-seen corridor in the distance. There was a faint musty smell of old unused houses.

Will whistled tunelessly. "Gosh. The Robot was right. Think mechanical, I gotta remember to ask for what I want instead of just worrying about it …"

Fearlessly he stepped forward down the ramp, and presently found himself at the intersection of a number of corridors.

"I wonder if I'll bump into Dad and Mom down here?" he said aloud. "Huh, machine?"

Nothing happened.

It was not a question the machine could formulate a response for. But the machine did run a check on its memory banks, searching for this being and then for its parents. Presently it recovered *in toto* all the information that had come to it since the Jupiter II had come within 17,400 miles of this planet's surface, which, among other things, included a record of every one of its passengers' conscious thoughts since that time.

Thus the machine obtained the information that this being's parents were walking through two parallel maintenance tunnels, almost directly away from his present position, at a distance of about 1400 *werts.* Absently the machine translated that into 1700 yards in the measuring-system of these newcomers.

For some minutes the boy descended the ramp system, until he was at last some six floors down from the surface.

"Maybe … maybe I should have stayed up on the first level," he thought. "There isn't anything down here. It's gonna be a long walk back up, too. Gee, I wish I had stayed with Mom and Dad …"

The machine digested this, decided it had enough information about these beings to translate that as a specific request, and then acted on its conclusion.

"Yipes!" explained Will. A panel in the wall of the corridor had suddenly *changed.*

Where it had been dull reddish-orange, a panel in the wall several feet wide and reaching to the ceiling had now become shimmery, as if a sort of gaseous mirror.

Will wondered for a moment whether he should run, then decided that if anything bad was going to happen to him, it would have happened by now. That left the problem of what it was.

Nervously he edged closer to the shimmering silvery surface, and, when nothing happened, dared to touch it gently.

There was no sensation.

It didn't hurt, it didn't not-hurt. There was no feeling of something being there. It was neutral. Intangible. The words tumbled through Will's mind, leftovers from lengthy sessions with his father, with Dr. Smith, with the Robot, as they all tried to cram as much of the abstract and practical knowledge of the human race into him as possible.

The words told him nothing, this time.

He shrugged his shoulders, and walked through the silvery shimmering.

He was face to face with his mother, who immediately screamed and slumped to the ground.

He jumped forward and caught her before she hurt herself. A signal came insistently over her communicator, and he detached it from his mother's waist gingerly.

"Maureen! Maureen! Are you all right? I'm almost there, darling–"

"Uh, Dad," he said into the communicator, his voice low and hesitant. "It's just me, Dad; everything's ok. I think. Maybe you better get here soon, though. I think, er, I think Mom has, er, fainted…"

"Where did–what have you–never mind, I'll be right there."

There was a decisive click from the communicator, and Will shrugged again. He was probably in for it now; why had he stepped through that wall? What a stupid thing to do! And now maybe Mother was hurt or something...

Maureen came to rather quickly, and found herself with her head cradled in her son's arms, a worried look on his face.

She smiled at him involuntarily. "Hi, son," she said, as cheerfully as she could, "I think everything's ok. But you gave me quite a start, whatever that was you did!"

"Gee, Mom, I'm awful sorry–it was–"

There was the sound of running footsteps, and John Robinson appeared at the next intersection.

"It's all right, John," Maureen called to him. But he ran towards her anyway. She tingled with warmth at the thought of how genuinely concerned he was; sometimes, with all the strains, she wondered whether he *could* possibly still feel the old emotions. It looked as if he somehow managed to... and she was pleased. *Her* emotions had not changed...

By the time Robinson got up to the two of them, Will spoke. "I figured out what I did, Dad," he said, immediately, before his father could bear down on him. "I found your subway. I think. Look here!"

Will stood up and walked to the corridor wall.

It was blank.

"Well," he said, "if it did it before, it can do it again. Hey, uh, machine. Could you do that again for me? I mean, do that with the wall?"

Nothing happened; after a moment Will snapped his fingers.

"Uh, machine, uh, can I go back to where I just was before?"

A panel of the dull reddish-orange wall changed into shimmering silvery nothingness...

"Oh, no," Maureen said a few minutes later. "You're not going jaunting about this city through those mirrors without me along. You've left me behind too many times."

Abruptly Robinson gave in. He had been trying to convince his wife that it was all right for him to use the newly discovered transportation system by himself. He realized she wouldn't give in, so he gave in.

"Come on, both of you," he said. "But it's back to where we started if we look like we're getting into any trouble."

He quickly realized that it was not going to be a very exciting trip.

Each time they went through the transporter field, they ended up in another corridor–and though the two spots were often as much as two hundred miles apart, the corridors always looked precisely the same.

"Wait a minute," he said, after the fourth journey had revealed only more corridors, "You, there, can you take us to any place that is *not* a corridor exactly like this one? I want to go to the nearest place like that, if such exists."

The transporter field evaporated into the wall.

The reddish-orange wall.

"Well, that's that," Robinson said. "Presumably this gadget will take us to the corridors under any building in this incredibly huge city, as we direct it. But we still have to walk upstairs to see the sights there.

"It'll help us get around, but it's not an answer in itself.

"Come on, Don must be–what was that?"

It was an alien, eerie whistling, and it echoed around them, beating in to them like the immediate ghost of a dead train...

"All right," said Judy. "We've learned that the sampling outlet here gives us frozen ... something, when we set the large knob here, and frozen ... something else, when we set it over here instead. I have an announcement. The large knob is *not* the temperature control!"

"Then that only leaves this other bank of pressure switches," Dan said.

"I'll have a baked alaska," Penny said, and laughed.

"You'll be lucky to get baked octopus, honey," Don said, and he laughed too.

"I'll settle for it being hot," said Judy. "I know we had to test every control systematically, to find out what did what, but I *do* wish we'd found the cooking controls sooner!..."

Don looked at the pressure-switches.

"Now the question is–do I throw the first one on the right, or the first one on the left? Which means just barely lit, and which one is full broil? Well, why don't I try–"

"Stop!" shrieked Judy. "Don't you have any sense? If you don't know which is hot and which is cold, hit the one in the middle, you ninny!"

Startled, Don looked up, then nodded. "Ok, I'll go along with that. I never did know much about the kitchen anyway. Here goes ..."

He stabbed a button, and nothing happened, for a moment.

Then an eerie whistling battered briefly at them, and after a moment, it came again, stronger, clearer– and more menacing ...

"There you are!" Smith announced triumphantly. "Just the very settings I wanted! And you–you pettifogging pincushion, you had no faith in me, no faith in me at all! Well, you see now that I, Smith, can do it! I can do anything I set my mind to. But you just criticize. So like a machine."

"You did a fine piece of work, Zachary," said the Robot, perhaps a trifle more tonelessly than usual. "Let's all hear it for Dr. Smith. Rah. Rah. Rah."

"Silence!" Dr. Smith said in his severest tones. "We move now to the next problem ... and what a lovely problem it is, too," he added with a chuckle.

"Simply the question of how best to utilize my new-found position at the precise center of the city's nervous system. What a vista of raw technology, all ready to do my bidding–whatever I want them to do! Ahhhh ... ."

And Smith set to work again, chancing settings, moving dials, adjusting calibrations, to the back-beat of an occasional, accidental heterodyne.

Then the first surge of the eerie whistling beat briefly into the room.

"Warning! Alien manifestation–extreme likelihood of imminent appearance of alien life form!"

"Nonsense," said Smith abstractedly, studying a complex image in the panel's screen. "Beastly noises. All about you constantly, won't let you alone. Penalty of living around machines, I suppose. A pity. But kindly don't bother me when I'm in the middle of important calculations, and ..."

During the last sentence the Robot broke in again, without Smith so much as turning and looking at him.

"Warning! Warning!"

The eerie whistling had returned, and this time it was getting louder, and louder, and louder ...

"Warning! Alien visitation immediate! Warning! Warning! ..."

The Robot was still shouting his futile warning when the ha-Grebst Raid-Chief laid his thick, hairy hand on the back of Dr. Zachary Smith's shoulder.

CHAPTER NINE

R aid-Chief Rethog of the ha-Grebst lashed his long hairy tail with impatience.

"Samarog, may the hair on your back smell sweet, and why in the name of the Holy Scar can't you get this ship off the ground and after that flier?"

"Oh, Great Chief, the smell of your fur is perfume in our nostrils, and the backphase turner was out of adjustment." And Samarog bent his seven-foot length in half at the waist in abasement for conveying negativistic information to a Raid-Chief of the ha-Grebst.

"Well, then, readjust the becursed turner and get us into the air, Samarog, before I call for the clippers." Rethog's tail, pleasantly odiferous–it had been fifty and more blessed nightfalls since the ship's Ritualizer, Scar his soul, had proclaimed a water-immersion day– curled about his feet. He knew Samarog would recognize that as the sign that Rethog was now only one step away from serious actions.

But Samarog's tail was twitching uncontrollably, indicating that he knew he could do no better–Scar him, too, and his tail that dared to be longer than Rethog's, and he'd better have a good excuse, Rethog thought.

"Your pardon, great Raid-Chief," murmured Samarog, "but when the main whiner-drive engines were turned on without a preliminary check on the frontphase and backphase tuners, the disruption caused by the backphase misalignment has caused damage that will take us until late afternoon to fix."

Rethog stared unwinkingly at his second-in-command and wondered whether to call for the clippers. A beep from his control panels caught his attention and he flipped a toggle. "Rethog. What's the scanning report?"

"Great Chief," came a voice over the intercom, "5th level emissions from the ship. That means faster-than-light capability, though the craft seemed small for interstellar journeys. Probability is that we observed only a scoutcraft. As evidence, the craft has already disappeared–in the direction from which it arrived," the voice continued hastily, sensing a burgeoning growl in Rethog's throat.

"And we're stuck with a whiner drive that needs six hours to fix. Very well." Rethog flipped the toggle and turned back to Samarog.

"Well, what are you doing here? Get to work on that Scar-filthy backphase tuner!"

Samarog scuttled out, leaving Rethog to broad over the mishaps of the past twenty-some nightfalls since they landed in this vast dead city.

First of all, no life at all–it had been 200 nightfalls since they'd raided their last planet, glutting the Great Scar with holy victims' blood.

Second of all, nothing worthwhile to plunder–so far, at least. In the approved ha-Grebst manner, he had done a quick mapping scan of the city, then had set to work examining the place block by block, starting from the outskirts and slowly expanding inwards. They'd discovered some interesting technological developments, but nothing of any great significance to the ha-Grebst. Unfortunately, they'd found enough that he had to continue the exploration, rather than whine back up for the stars and another planet with more interesting characteristics.

Third, the alien scoutcraft–a defenseless morsel, yet as safe from his ship as from a Scar-cursed raindrop, since the *Djengl,* it seemed, wasn't going to move for another quarterday.

It didn't improve his disposition when, several hours later, the scanners picked up a larger ship, with definite 6th level emissions leaking from the ship.

"Great Chief, it is not only faster-than-light, it is jump-ship class, with intergalactic range. And excellent news–the ship is operating under some grave disability. It may be simply putting in here for repairs!"

"Ahhhhhh," said Raid-Chief Rethog, and slumped back into his hammock, scratching the tip of his tail with one of the rat-like fangs in his rat-like face and growling with pleasure. "Things go ill *my* way for a change," he said.

There was the sound of a tail slapping on the deck outside his cabin entrance. "Enter," he said, responding to the knock.

It was Samarog. "We can take off at the end of the hour," he announced, proud at having shaved the time by a factor of one fourth.

"One hour, then," said Rethog, "and Scar save you if the ship doesn't lift."

But the *Djengl* did lift, its magnadrive emitting the characteristic whining whistle that gave it the nickname 'whiner-drive'.

Quickly the *Djengl* approached the central plaza, where his instruments told Rethog the newcomers had already dispersed from their ship.

He put his spherical craft down in a smaller nearby plaza, the magnadrive shrieking even louder at touchdown.

A side of the *Djengl* swung to one side, and the ha-Grebst raiding party emerged on a scoutsled, with its own smaller magnadrive unit shrieking and whistling even louder, with the effort of converting helium to controlled energy pulses.

Quickly the raiding sled shot to the top of the two-mile-high Central Tower, where Rethog's instruments indicated one of the aliens was investigating certain highly complex–and highly interesting– computer controls.

It took only seconds to burn through the roof-surface and descend to the door of the room where the alien was adjusting controls.

"Burn the door," Rethog commanded. He hated the mental effort it took to open the Scar-cursed things anyway.

Quickly and silently one of the ha-Grebst burned out the door, and Raid-Chief Rethog entered the room.

Ignoring the Robot, which to the ha-Grebst seemed only to be a mobile computer, neither alive nor even conscious, Rethog made for the repulsive alien figure that was sitting with his back to him.

The alien was unexpectedly strong, and fought him off long enough to shout cryptically into what Rethog assumed, quite correctly, was a device to communicate with his fellows.

"Aliens!" came Smith's voice urgently over the communicator. "Huge ugly hairy things! Armed! Help! Hel–"

The communicator fell silent.

"Smith? Smith!" shouted Robinson into his communicator. "Come in! Answer me! Are you all right?"

Silence.

"Come on," he said to the others in the food-production building. "We've got to rescue him– quick!"

They dashed across the deep blue lake of the plaza, and into the Central Tower.

The anti-gravity beam deposited the six, one by one and weapons ready, at the top floor several minutes later.

Smith stood in the doorway to the computer room, looking haggard and nervous.

"Put your weapons away," he said. "We must leave this place."

"What!" said Robinson angrily.

"They have voder translators, and we have talked. They are this city's owners. You can join us now, Rethog. I believe they are ready to listen to you."

Dubiously, Robinson pocketed his laser and indicated that the rest should spread out but also put away their pistols.

Through the doorway strode a seven-foot-tall monster–such at least was Robinson's immediate reaction. Rat-like face, hair everywhere, thick and shaggy. Odor of animal sweat and rotten food–*strong* odor. Robinson almost gagged, and the girls were pale with shock at the stench.

Rat-face spoke, uttering growls which were immediately translated into toneless English by a machine at his waist.

"I am Raid-Chief Rethog, of the ha-Grebst. This is our city you are despoiling. You must leave immediately. Now. Take nothing. Leave immediately." The mechanical voice fell silent.

"We…"

Robinson paused and searched for words. The stench was growing stronger and stronger. Behind the Raid-Chief he could see others of the rat-faced, hairy aliens; and off to one side, completely ignored, stood the Jupiter's Robot, silent, motionless. "Have they destroyed him?" he thought in sudden anxiety.

"We are sorry to have intruded upon your territory, Robinson said aloud, slowly. "We will leave as soon as we repair our instruments and replenish our fuel supply.

Perhaps you could even help us; the sooner we are able to go, the sooner we will go. We would also like food, but–"

It was an odd distraction to hear the voder translator rendering his voice in alien growlings; then Rethog interrupted him with curt snarls.

"No food. No fuel. You must leave now. How you leave is your affair, but *you must leave.*"

And rat-face reached for an odd device at his waist.

"Hit the floor!" Robinson shouted. "That's a weapon he's got there, I'm sure of it." A glance showed everyone dodging for safety, and he concentrated on the alien.

"It is a weapon," stated the toneless voder, as ratface extended it in Robinson's direction. "You will leave."

There was a movement behind Rethog, and he turned his head slightly. His rat-like bulging eyes saw the Robot moving towards him, and he started to turn his weapon towards this new threat.

There was a sharp crackling sound, and twin bolts of force shot from the Robot's pincer-like metal hands. The bolts struck the alien weapon, and Rethog yowled with sudden pain, dropping the weapon at the same time.

"Fire if they draw another weapon," Robinson shouted, as the Robot attempted to block the doorway and prevent the rest of the ha-Grebst from reaching the humans.

There was a low hum, and part of the wall beside the Robot erupted outwards towards the humans.

Maureen and Penny dodged behind a pillar, while Don and Robinson aimed their laser pistols at the new opening, waiting for something to show in the clouds of dust.

"Will! Judy!" Robinson looked about, and saw his son behind another pillar.

There was a clanging, insistant sound from the doorway.

Several ha-Grebst in the computer room were piling up on the Robot, trying to topple him over– Robinson moved his laser to pick one off–a dart of movement– others were coming through the hole in the wall–he swerved his laser again and winged several–everything quick, quick movements, quick judgments–and nobody to complain to if the judgment was incorrect...

Robinson wiped sweat from his brow, as there was another crackle from the Robot's metal hands. A billow of dense smoke was pouring out from his chest cavity, and Robinson grinned. A simple smoke bomb.

The Earthmen's fire and the smoke from the Robot were too much for Raid-Chief Rethog. One of the aliens had been grabbed–excellent, that would do for now. Too bad it wasn't that odd one by the computer, but...

Rethog bellowed to his men to take to the raiding-sled, as he stumbled through the smoke and into the Robot. Cursing, he broke away from the clumsy monstrosity with the aid of strong ha-Grebst arms hauling him around it.

As they retreated, several of the ha-Grebst took snap shots at the Earthmen, but they were rattled now, and the pale blue rays sizzled harmlessly into walls and floor, etching deep burns in whatever they touched.

The clouds of smoke grew thicker, and it was almost impossible to see. Shouts and growls of alarm and command crossed each other as both sides tried to assess and take charge of the situation.

Then there was a distant scream, and a burst of blue light in the computer room.

The ha-Grebst had retreated through the roof; there was a sharp whining whistle, and the raiding-sled was airborne and away from the Central Tower . . .

As the smoke began to disperse through the new hole in the roof the ha-Grebst had created for their escape, Robinson looked about to assess the results of the conflict.

"Judy!" shouted Don in anguish. "They got Judy!"

"Oh, no," whispered Maureen. "Is she . . . is she dead?"

"No," said Don. "They grabbed her–took her with them. In all the smoke and confusion I lost track of her, then I saw one of them holding her as he was helped on to some sort of mobile sled thing they took off on."

"Great," said Robinson bitterly.

"You know," mused Don, "I don't think those beasts *are* the owners of this city. Why would they kidnap one of us? It doesn't make any sense. They don't need a bargaining point with us. all they need is to just kick us out. And if they were really the people who built this place, I don't think they'd have any trouble at all getting rid of us."

"You've got a point," Robinson agreed, eager to take his mind off his daughter for a moment, "And why should they go around burning holes in their own ceilings? It doesn't make sense."

"So what do we do about Judy," demanded Maureen. "When and how do we get her back?"

"Frankly, I don't know," Robinson answered. "But if those things could easily get rid of us, they would. My conclusion is that they can't. But I don't know whether we can get rid of them, either. And they have Judy, so we can't just blast their ship, assuming we can even find it."

"Well, you're going to do *something,* aren't you?" his wife insisted.

"Yes–but what? If we could just find some advanced weapons here, something that could give us an edge ... I have a feeling we'll hear from them pretty soon. In the meantime ..." He shrugged, his face as miserable as his feelings inside. "Well, all I can say is–spread out again, and let's see what we can find."

"Hey, what about Smith?" There was a deep note of suspicion in Don's voice. "What was he doing up here that made them come here in the first place? In fact, where did he go?"

"Did they get him too?"

"*I* didn't see anything."

"Did I hear my name?" It was Smith.

"Where did you go?" demanded Don. "When the action started, I mean."

" 'The better part of valor is discretion,' the immortal Bard has stated. My weapon having been purloined by one of those disreputable and smelly beasts, I sought a vantage point of safety in the confusion."

"Ok, ok," said Don. "Catch you with your excuses down, I suppose that'd be the day. I don't suppose you have any worthwhile ideas on what we should do to find Judy?"

Smith looked pious. "I was learning a few things about the computer system here when I was so rudely interrupted. My feeling is that I can continue to serve at my most useful by remaining here pursuing the lines I had been working on ..."

"Fine," said Robinson, cutting him off. "Let us know if you get anything from these panels here. They look pretty fancy. I hope they didn't get too badly banged up in the fracas, but they look pretty sturdy. You're the computer expert, Dr. Smith, make like an expert– and fast. We want Judy back, and quickly."

"Very well," Smith answered, drawing himself up. "Never fear, Smith is here. I shall endeavor to exert my fullest intellectual–"

"Action, not talk, Smith," said Don harshly. "Just figure these panels out and help find a way to get her back."

"Hmph," said Smith, and re-seated himself at one of the consoles with an air of disdain, ignoring the others.

"Oh, John, what if we can't get her back?" said Maureen, and she clung to his chest for a moment, her tears warm and wet on his shirt. "What ... if we've lost her ... forever? Those *horrible* rat-faced monsters! ..."

Robinson patted her on the back and tried to comfort her.

"Now, Maureen, it's going to be all right. Let's leave Dr. Smith here to do what he can, and go back down to that information panel on the ground floor. If we work at it, maybe we can locate a weapons depot, or something…"

Smith turned to watch them as they stepped one by one onto the down-plate of the anti-gravity beam, and as soon as Don, the last, disappeared, he jumped up and rubbed his hands with glee.

"Ah, yes," he chuckled to himself, "Smith is here. Among a whole new world of goodies. Now for that other room. How fortunate I fell against it and begged– er, asked, for it to open. I don't think I would have suspected it was here…"

He crossed the room to a bare wall panel, and waved a hand at it. Obeying his silent thought, it opened into a door, and he walked into the second room.

"Hmmm. now let's see. Yes, these machines *are* different from the other room," he mused aloud. "Perhaps it will take me a little more time than I had anticipated, to penetrate these mysteries.

"Now what's this thing?"

A transparent panel was inset into the largest panel board in the room. Inside was what looked like nothing so much as a lady's hair-net, but made out of silvery-gleaming lustrous wires.

He fiddled with the transparent panel a moment, till it slid aside; then he reached in and drew out the silvery net.

"Not attached to anything else; what in heaven's name can this thing be for?"

He ran his hands over the wires and studied the points at which the silvery wires intersected each other.

"Curious," he said. "Little weight to the thing, but a feeling of strength. And it's hard to focus my eyes on the intersections…"

He hefted it again, and then on impulse opened it out and placed it on his head.

Absolutely nothing happened.

Smith shrugged, and looked about for something to plug the net into–when there was a thud on the floor behind him.

He turned instantly–to face a seven-foot-tall ha-Grebst warrior crouched under the hole he had obviously just burned in the roof.

"Left one behind up there, eh?" Smith said, surprised at his own coolness.

The ha-Grebst crouched lower and growled. "One by one, Earthman," the voder translator said. "You cannot escape."

And with that the rat-faced alien lunged for Smith.

But the ha-Grebst was slow and clumsy by Earth standards, and Smith evaded his first attack easily. As the ha-Grebst brushed by him, Smith gagged on the rank stench, and wondered why the filthy beast didn't just blast him with his ray gun.

"Ha!" Smith said, and tugged for the spare laser Robinson had handed him before the others had left. "Sometimes I forget myself."

The alien growled hideously, and one claw-like hand swept the laser from Smith's smaller hand.

"No weapons," the ha-Grebst snarled. "Feel you die under my own fangs." And the ha-Grebst lunged again.

As Smith evaded him again, his back bumped against a chair, and, knocked off-balance, he fell to the floor heavily. Instantly the ha-Grebst whirled about and prepared to pounce on the helpless Earthman.

"Stop!" shrieked Smith, in terror of his life. "Oh, please, stay back–stay there–don't come any closer!"

He squeezed his eyes shut in anticipation of the awful end that was fast approaching him, and his mind gibbered on and on, begging, pleading, ordering the ha-Grebst not to kill him. His breath ran out and he sucked in fresh oxygen–and Grebst-stink– greedily and fearfully.

A moment passed; another moment. Seconds now, five, ten ...

Fearfully, Smith opened one eye.

The ha-Grebst was poised above him, mouth agape, fangs dripping a foul slime.

"No, no," Smith shrieked aloud. "Go away–get away from me!"

Before he could close his eyes again, the astonished Smith saw the ha-Grebst abruptly begin backpedalling as fast as he could, directly away from the prostrate man, until his back fetched up against the far wall, whereupon the ha-Grebst stopped with one foot still up in the air, motionless.

"Wha–" Smith began, then stopped.

He peered at the motionless alien more closely.

The ha-Grebst was in a rigid, almost catatonically quiet state, his arms and legs frozen in what, even to the Earthman's uncertain, ignorant eye, were obviously unnatural positions.

Smith was a coward first, perhaps, but a scientist second, and as his fear slowly left him, his mind began searching for answers.

"Why...why are you standing like that?" he said slowly to the rigid ha-Grebst.

"You told me to get away from you. I can go no further without further directions." The snarls were bitten off, clipped; the voder was as toneless as ever.

"*I* told you? But–"

Smith fell silent, then realized that the ha-Grebst might come out of his strange inactive state at any moment. Frantically he scrabbled around on the floor for his laser pistol, and found it just in time to turn around– and see the ha-Grebst slowly lowering one hairy leg and begin to move forward even more slowly.

"Oh, no, you foul-smelling rodent," Smith said triumphantly, waving the laser in the air with a grand gesture. "You just stay where you are and answer my questions."

The ha-Grebst froze once more.

"Um," said Smith, indecisive about what to ask.

The ha-Grebst remained motionless.

Absently, Smith started to scratch his head–and felt the silvery network of thin wires, still in place over his thin hair.

"Aha!" Smith shouted. "So that's it! Are you obeying me because of this thing on my head?"

"I do not know," the ha-Grebst voder said.

"No, no, no, it must be the network, you ignoramus. It's some sort of headset, a control unit, something to do with the computers..."

Experimentally, Smith slowly began to lift the headset from his skull.

Nothing happened–until it was completely away from his head.

With a fierce growl that overrode the voder's futile attempt at translation, the ha-Grebst charged toward Smith from the far wall.

"Woops!" Smith said, and clapped the headset firmly back on his head once more. "Stop right there, fellow! This is Smith speaking, and don't you forget it!"

The ha-Grebst froze once more.

Smith smiled.

Smith grinned.

Smith chuckled, laughed aloud, then broke into hysterical giggles ...

"I've found it!" he choked out finally, almost hysterical with glee, and he did a little skip-step.

"Why, I can't believe it! All my life I've searched for the key, the key to conquest, to power, to glory, the key by which I could attain all my deepest dreams–and now ..." His voice fell to a hush. "And now ... I've found it!"

His manic laughter increased again.

Helpless with laughter at last, he stumbled over to a seat and eased himself into it, then relaxed and let the wild feeling of elation and joy surge through him, touching every nerve in his body with sheer anticipatory delight ...

There was a movement from the ha-Grebst. Toward Smith. The motion caught his eye.

"Oh, no, my fine fellow," Smith said imperiously. "You just forget about ever thinking for yourself, my boy. You're mine now. You, my incredibly ugly friend, you …"

He struggled to express all his feelings at once, then found one paramount emotion surging outwards. "Yes!" he shouted with delight.

"You–kneel before me, first of my subjects. For I shall become King Zachary–no. No, grander than that–Emperor Zachary the First. The only! Ruler of the world–ruler of the galaxy! Power–power in my hands at last! Power to rule …

"Power to rule … the universel" His voice had sunk to a whisper, as his mind drifted off to thoughts of the adamantine throne he would have constructed to his precise directions–it would be chased with the rarest diamonds embedded in purest gold. His palace would be constructed of one block of stone each from every planet under his iron sway, with every precious gem and metal represented in his dominions studded into the walls, an endless gleaming tribute to his power and sway …

Emperor Zachary! Tears of gratitude for his immeasurable luck–and great skill–coursed down his cheeks as he contemplated that which was to be …

CHAPTER TEN

"**W**arning! Warning!" the Robot intoned, as he rolled along beside Will through the corridors under the Central Tower. "My sensors indicate we are approaching a source of immense, perhaps virtually immeasurable power. Warning! I cannot assist you against such strength! Will Robinson, you should return at once to your parents–"

"Shush," said Will firmly. "If we all don't take a few chances we're all going to end up like Judy. Besides, power is just what we want now, you know that. We've got to get her back from those awful rat-men!"

"The ha-Grebst are a race of great power," said the Robot. "Perhaps it would be wisest to do as they say ..."

Will stopped in his tracks and stared at the Robot.

"Why–why, I never knew you were a *coward*, Robot!" he said, almost breathlessly.

"No, Will Robinson, I am not a coward. But I am a realist. There is danger here in these corridors, I am certain of it–great danger. Even the ha-Grebst are almost certainly less dangerous. Hence: perhaps the ha-Grebst are our only chance of surviving."

Will shook his head firmly. "No, Robot. We must keep going. We must have hope. Without hope …"

He choked, and thought of that last glimpse of Judy, her face contorted with fear and loathing as one of the ha-Grebst hauled her up through the hole in the ceiling …

"Hope," said the Robot, whirring and clicking. "Hope does not compute. But–good luck, Will Robinson. I will stay with you and do what I can."

Will smiled at the Robot and patted him on the arm. "Thanks, Robot. I knew you were ok. You always have come through in the pinch. You're swell, you know that?"

"Swell does not compute, Will Robinson. But thank you anyway."

Will grinned to himself. That darned Robot was always pretending he didn't understand what human beings were all about–but he was more human than most people he'd ever known!

They were nine levels down from the surface now, and he could see no indication that any of the levels so far had differed from any of the others.

"How come they need so many levels for their maintenance machines, like Dad said this was all for?" he asked the Robot, not really expecting an answer.

"Perhaps this city has had other uses for them after all. I cannot say. As your mother said, aliens are … alien, Without the aliens to tell us, therefore, it is doubtful that we will ever learn more than a fraction of the secrets bidden in this city. And would they tell us, even if we asked?"

"Yeah," said Will. "I see what you mean, I guess. Well, here's another ramp. Come on, Robot, we gotta keep on going. Is that feeling of danger getting any stronger?"

"Yes, Will Robinson," said the Robot, as its foot-track motors whined momentarily at the strain of keeping him down to the boy's pace on the ramp's slope.

"Among other things, I can tell you at this point that this ramp is steeper than the ones we have been traversing. I suspect this may be an older section of the city that we are now visiting."

"Yes," said Will excitedly, as they reached the foot of the ramp. "The walls are brown, here! And the corridor is narrower, and the ceiling's not as high! Come on, let's see if there's another ramp!"

They doubled back past the bulk of the ramp, looking for the next one directly underneath it, just as with the nine levels above this one.

But there was no ramp.

"Warning! Danger!" said the Robot. "Manifestations of great power are closer than ever! But," the Robot added unexpectedly, "I suppose that does not make any difference. I suggest, therefore, that we take the corridor to the left. That is where I receive the strongest impression of power."

They walked in silence for several minutes, until Will spoke suddenly.

"Hey! Hey, I hear my footsteps echoing! They aren't using that absorbent field down here along these corridors. We *must* be close to finding something out!"

"Affirmative. Strong fields of power on this level have negated the protective field that extends throughout the rest of the city.

"There is a door in the wall just ahead of us," the Robot continued. "A solid door, I mean; not one of those dilating doors we have found elsewhere.

"And my sensors report that behind it lies the source of great power I have been sensing for the past ten minutes."

They approached the panel in the wall. A small square of white material, crisscrossed with thin black lines, was set at one side of the panel, well above Will's head.

"Push that, will you, Robot," asked Will. "I bet that's the doorbell."

He almost laughed at the thought, then fell silent, feeling sweat on the palms of his hands. *Maybe we should go back!*–the thought screamed in his mind, but he stood there resolutely, remembering Judy, as the Robot extended his arm and touched the white square.

The wall panel shimmered for a moment like one of the matter transmitters, then vanished.

Beyond the empty doorway was a vast room, filled with giant circular vats, extending as far as Will could see into distant dimness. Low illumination showed a short ramp, which led downward from the door to the floor of the huge room some twenty feet below the level of the corridor floor.

"It … it looks like a brewery," Will said at last in a whisper. "Robot, what … what does it mean?"

"The source of great power is within this room, Will Robinson," said the Robot. "Apart from that, I know no more than you do."

"Ok," said Will, and shrugged. "Let's go on inside…"

His footsteps echoed as he strode manfully down the ramp, ignoring his fears.

"I got used to not hearing my footsteps," he said to the Robot. "Their echoes, I mean. Now they make me nervous…" He giggled for a moment, then fell silent again.

They reached the floor of the huge room, and looked up at the nearest vat, its top some forty feet above them. Its steel-like sides gleamed dully in the dim light of the room.

A set of hand-holds, twice as big and twice as far apart as humans would build, ran up the side of the vat to the top.

"I'm going up," Will said decisively. "It's the only thing to do. We've got to know what's inside."

"Very well, Will Robinson. But…there is great danger. I…I want you to know…that if anything happens…I will miss you very much…"

The Robot fell silent, and Will could sense his embarrassment–impossible in a robot, but indisputably there.

Will choked, and patted the Robot on the arm.

Then he reached up to the first handhold, and began hoisting himself up.

By the time he had reached the rung just below rim, he was panting for breath, and the sweat was rolling down his back. He paused at the rim, looking down at the foreshortened Robot far below him.

Then he peered over the rim.

A giant, naked, sexless body twice as tall as a man floated in a dark soupy fluid.

Eyes closed, the hairless giant lay motionless, only the front of its body showing above the fluid, but with its head propped up by something so that the face seemed to be staring sightlessly, straight at ten-year-old William Robinson of Earth.

The eyes opened, and blinked at the boy …

"Dance, Traggon, dance," shouted Smith with delight as they emerged from the Central Tower into the late afternoon sunlight.

The ha-Grebst, absolute captive of the silvery headset, pranced and danced in awkward alien hops, as the two proceeded toward the *Djengl.*

"Tut-tut," Smith said, observing the clumsy antics of his new slave, "surely you can dance better than that?"

"Dancing not ha-Grebst concept," said Traggon slowly, forced by the headset to conceptualize thoughts so alien to him that his head would have hurt if it had still been under his control. "Closest thing is antics of very youthful ha-Grebst, before learning ha-Grebst way."

"Hmmm," Smith said. As the alien spoke of the 'ha-Grebst way,' Smith had picked up a surge from his mind involuntarily defining it. It was not a pretty thing, the ha-Grebst teaching method. There was a lot in that flash from Traggon's mind about whips, and electric shocks, and other, more formless horrors. With the flash came something of an insight into the ha-Grebst mind, however: an utterly feral, insensately ferocious natural attitude that could only be kept under control by the most savage kind of conditioning.

Smith shook his head as if to dislodge the images of pain and bestiality. "This mind-controlling business isn't all it's cracked up to be," he thought. "But I shall make do, in my customary indomitable manner."

They rounded a corner and the ha-Grebst raiding-craft loomed before them, its spherical bulk almost completely filling the width of the small plaza it sat in.

"Phew," said Smith. "What a reek around that thing! Tell me, my unwashed lad, do you have H_2O on your wretched planet?" "Yes."

"Well, then, why in thunderation don't you ever use it on yourselves?"

"We do. Once a *porlan,* whether we need it or not. Or more frequently, if the ship's Ritualizer proclaims a water-immersion day. It is the ha-Grebst way."

Once again Smith received an image directly from Traggon's mind; a *porlan,* it seemed, was something on the order of 144 days, though it was difficult to be sure how long a ha-Grebst day was.

"Well," Smith said, "that certainly explains *that.* When my new order becomes fully established, I believe that will be one of the first things I shall see to changing. Do you hear that, you misbegotten fugitive from a garbage heap? I shall introduce regular bathing to your people, and a new joy in life shall be yours!"

The alien snarled.

"I heard that, Traggon. We'll have no more of that. Now. How do we get inside this contraption?"

Traggon reached up to the side of the raider-craft and half-twisted a small disk set in the *Djengl's* hull.

With a harsh sawing sound, a steep ramp extended outwards and downwards from the ship, and a panel slid aside. In the opening stood another ha-Grebst.

The new ha-Grebst snarled at Traggon.

A slow smile grew on Smith's face. The headset was translating every word for him–which was fortunate, because the ha-Grebst did not have his voder translator on.

"I heard that, Rethog," Smith said. "I hear everything. And I shall answer instead of your compatriot here, who is no longer answering any questions but those I pose him. No, Rethog, I am not his prisoner. He is mine.

"And so are you."

Raid-Chief Rethog snarled and took one step forward–and froze in mid-step.

The smile on Smith's face grew broader.

"Ahhhh. How easy it is for a superior mind to impress his inferiors." He thought a moment.

"Order all your men to come out here and–no, wait. I'll do it myself."

Smith's face creased in concentration, as he formed a mental order for the rest of the ha-Grebst to appear–and then he remembered Judy, and ordered them to bring her out too.

Moments later they began appearing, walking hesitantly at first, then more firmly as Smith's mind grew more adept at its task.

With the last two of the twelve rat-faced aliens was Judy, looking pale.

"Dr. Smith!" she gasped. "They caught you too! Are– are the others all right?"

"They are perfectly well, so far as I know, my dear," he answered unctuously. "And as you will see, so am I!"

He concentrated on a series of mental commands then.

The twelve ha-Grebst silently grouped themselves in a circle on the small plaza, in the deep afternoon shadow of their raider-craft.

Then they all joined hands and, with extreme awkwardness, began to dance around in a circle...

Judy's mouth gaped in stunned wonderment.

Smith chuckled indulgently. "A. mere nothing. Watch now!"

The ha-Grebst ceased their cumbersome dancing, squatted down on the plaza, and, slowly, deliberately, stood on their heads, propping themselves up with varying degrees of success with their claw-like hands...

Smith clapped his hands, and they all resumed their upright positions.

"What else would you like me to have them do, my dear–as, let us say, a penance for having the temerity to take prisoner a friend of Dr. Zachary Smith?" He was in his element now, and he both knew it and relished it thoroughly.

She had to make several attempts at speaking before intelligent sounds came out. "What...why...why are they doing that?"

"Ah, now," Smith said triumphantly, smugly, "that will be my little secret.

"But I will tell you that I can make them do whatever I want them to do, from now on. And the first thing I shall do is to use my power to get us off this planet. I have found what I wanted–what I have *always* wanted. Power!

"Yes, my dear, from now on the story of Smith the man shall be transformed into the story of Smith the king–Smith the Emperor!"

A thought struck him, and he brightened even more.

"And you may, if you wish, become my first Empress– once I've got things running properly under my control, that is. Even with my power, I shall have to proceed with a certain amount of care. As someone or other has said, these things must be done delicately…"

Regaining some of her composure, Judy said forth-rightly, "Dr. Smith, I don't understand. Could you explain all this more clearly? What do you mean, Emperor–and Empress? What makes you think I want to be an Empress, too–especially your Empress?"

Smith's face darkened.

"My dear, with the control device … hm, we won't go into that. At any rate, I can make anyone–or any *thing,* such as these loathsome unwashed beasts I have had cavorting for your amusement–do precisely what I order them to do. My intentions are simple. I shall take over their planet, and their planet's possessions, and then I shall expand my influence. I should imagine that within, oh, a few months, I shall have a nice little interstellar empire going, and I assure you I shall proceed to expand its boundaries to the limits of this marvelous machine's capabilities. Why, the possibilities are endless!"

Judy's eyes widened. "Dr. *Smith!* You wouldn't–"

"Ho, ho, ho!" Smith said. "Just watch me!"

"I'll have nothing to do with your mad plans," she said decisively. "You can have all these smelly beasts if you want to, but *I'm* going back to the Jupiter."

And she strode purposefully down the ramp and past Smith.

"'That's what you think," Smith muttered, scowling. He shot a mental command at her–and she kept walking!

"What the–" said aloud, astonished. Already he could see his dreams of conquest fading. "No, I won't accept it, I *won't!* My beautiful empire!" he wailed.

Judy kept walking.

"*Stop!*" he shouted at her–and breathed a sigh of relief.

Judy had frozen in mid-step.

"Now, come back here," Smith said aloud. She turned and walked woodenly toward him.

"I can see this gadget is going to take some time getting used to," he grumbled. "Why didn't you come the first time?"

"The first time? I only heard you call once," she said, as expressionlessly as one of the ha-Grebst voder translators.

He scowled, then brightened immediately. "I have it! The first time I controlled a ha-Grebst. it was a vocal command that preceded it–and it was the same with you. Yes! Very likely it takes that much for the head-set to establish neurological resonance with a given race; then after that, a mental command alone ... After all, to whomever *really* owns this city, we are both alien races." He didn't bother to explain to her that the moment he'd first touched Traggon's mind, he'd learned the ha-Grebst were aliens to this planet, just like Earthmen.

"Well, that's no longer important; I'm tuned to both races now."

He thought about that for a moment, then turned decisively to the ha-Grebst, who were standing exactly as he had left them.

The sight pleased him; obviously he was getting the hang of controlling people with the headset. Fortunately, less immediate concentration on each individual seemed to be required, the longer they remained under his control.

"That's fortunate for my plans, if so," he mused aloud. "I hadn't considered how difficult it might be to be constantly giving commands one by one–to a whole planetful of people!"

"Hmmm, people. Perhaps we'd all better just go along now and look up the rest of the Robinson family."

Smith stood up straighter, hummed a little tune, and smoothed his tunic.

"Now, my beautiful cohorts, follow me! Work to do, work to do! March now–hut, two three, four, hut two–"

And twelve ha-Grebst and one Earth girl fell into step behind him ...

"I think we've found what we're looking for," Will had shouted down to the Robot. "Why don't you call Dad and the others and get them all down here?"

The Robot had complied, and a few minutes later the crew of the Jupiter II–less Judy and Dr. Smith– were crowding in through the doorway to the room of the vats.

They were just in time to see a twelve-foot-high, naked, sexless, hairless being climb very slowly down out of one of the vats.

Will called to them excitedly.

"Come on, come on, Dad, I don't think he's danger-ous," he was shouting.

"*He?*" Maureen said half-aloud, as the being reached the bottom and turned to face them all. "How can you possibly tell?"

The giant being began going into what were obvi-ously a form of isometric calesthenics–a slow pattern of stretchings and tensings of its magnificent muscles which continued for several minutes while the Earth people stood in silent awe, watching.

Then the giant stopped, and peered closely at Will, his hairless brows knitting slightly.

"Eng-lish," he said at last, slowly. "Am I … to pre-sume … that … you all … speak this rudimentary … spo-ken tongue?"

The voice was a pleasant baritone, with overtones and resonances that gave an odd, but not unpleasant, twang to his speech.

"That's right," Robinson said, stepping forward. "And I presume that you are of the race that built this city?"

"The … city." The giant blinked several times.

"You must … pardon me. I have been here for … some time. It is … difficult to speak … even to think … waking up after … so many years."

The giant closed his eyes and turned his head from side to side several times, slowly, then opened hiseyes and looked at them again.

"So it is … my turn at last … to supervise."

"Supervise?"

"It is a … long story," the giant said.

Suddenly the expressionless face was creased with a faint smile. "A longer story … than you could dream.

"Dream!"

With the repetition of the word, the smile vanished from his face, and he shook his head again from side to side a few more times.

"Such dreams … such dreams I've had," he said then. "Better than waking … far, far better. I think that I shall go back to sleep again after the … proving, even if … you are the Worthy Ones."

The Earth people could almost hear the capital letters in the last two words.

Then the giant seemed to remember something, and strode slowly over to the nearest wall. He pressed a white square in it, and the wall lit up with an intricately cryptic diagram which the giant studied carefully for several minutes in silence.

"All is well, then, with Giandahar," he said. "The city stands, and my people remain … asleep.

"But many have visited Giandahar since first I fell into my dream-rich sleep, and all have left again."

He sighed. "And still do we await ... the Worthy Ones."

"How ... how many of you are there, asleep down here in these gigantic vats?" Robinson asked, and realized as he spoke that he was little more than whispering, with the awe of what they were seeing.

"Alas," the giant said with sadness in his voice, "little more than a ... million of us decided to await the Worthy Ones. The rest have been dead since before we placed ourselves in the nutrient vats ..."

"And how long have you yourself been sleeping?" Robinson continued, determined to try to begin to make coherent sense out of what was happening.

The giant turned to the glowing wall, and cryptic squiggles flashed across it.

"So *very* long?" he said, and shook his head a third time.

"I have been sleeping here ... for seven billion years."

CHAPTER ELEVEN

There was a ringing sound in Robinson's ears, and then he heard his wife's voice calling his name alarmedly.

"John, John, are you all right?"

He realized that he had half-slumped to the floor and that she had held him from falling completely over.

"I–I guess so. Guess I've been under … too much on my mind, lately. Strain."

"*I'll* say," she announced maternally. "You haven't even had anything to eat since breakfast and it's almost night time. Have a bite of emergency rations, John. They may not taste good, but they'll do you good."

He munched on the biscuit in his pack and began to feel better.

During this, the giant had turned away politely and was studying his arcane wall-charts.

Robinson decided his head was clear again, and spoke. "Uh, I'm sorry. Bit too many shocks too quickly, I believe."

"You find my story hard to believe already, do you not?" the giant said.

"No," Robinson answered firmly, which made the giant look at him with greater interest. "No, it's just because I *do* believe you, I think, that made me dizzy for a moment. I don't think the idea's preposterous because I've seen your city.

"I've seen many things in the past two years. The galaxy is big, and it is old. And much is strange past my understanding; not, however, past my belief.

"That is, assuming you can explain."

"Two other members of your race are on the surface," said the giant obliquely. "And a dozen members of a failed race."

It was Robinson's turn to shake his head, in puzzlement. "The ha-Grebst? You move too fast for me. Er. ... By the way, what name should we call you by?"

The giant smiled. "You change your thoughts even as you speak, yet you complain when I do much the same. The life-force still breeds true. You may call me Gil-mish. It is a symbolic rendition in your tongue of my Giandhu name, which exists only as a pure thought construct and is not capable of being directly verbalized."

Don blew air through his pursed lips, but could not whistle.

Maureen spoke up, rather surprised at the sharpness of her tone. "One of those humans up on the surface is my daughter, Gil'mish. She is a prisoner of ... I suppose those you called a 'failed race.' Is she safe? Can you help her?"

Gil'mish passed a hand over his smooth broad forehead.

"I … I am certain she will be safe … for the time being. You must, however … pardon me. I remain temporarily … weak with reaction to my awakening. It may take me a few small units of your time … till I am fully myself. Then we shall see about the failed ones."

"Very well," said Robinson. "We accept that; after all, we are uninvited guests here in the first place. Maureen, I'm sure that with what we've seen, we needn't fear that Gil'mish is capable of helping us. And I'm sure that he will when he can."

"Thank you," Gil'mish said, and nodded. "But I must assure you, you are hardly uninvited guests.

"You were supposed to come here."

"*Supposed* to!" said Don. "I quit. This is beyond me."

"Pardon, that is not quite accurate. I meant that all are welcomed here, who are capable of getting here."

"Including the ha-Grebst? They were in process of systematically looting this place when we arrived. How do you keep such people from making off with everything–" Robinson laughed in spite of himself "–especially since, as you said, you've been asleep for … seven billion years."

"We have our methods. This history screen tells me nothing has happened that cannot be repaired.

"Over thirty thousand times in the period since the Giandhu chose to sleep has one of us been awakened– each time, the city has seen to it that a different one was wakened, incidentally, for that was what we all agreed upon. Hopefully, none of us will have to waken more than once before we waken for the last time, all of us, to greet the Worthy Ones."

The Robot whirred and clicked. "For your information, Professor Robinson, that indicates that the Giandhu apparently were prepared to sleep here for well over two hundred billion years. This figure is far beyond that date established as the probable time of the final energy death of the entire universe. Suggestion: take Gil'mish's statements with a small quantity of sodium chloride. Hrrrmmm. That is, a grain of salt."

"Your science is in error," Gil-mish said gravely. "I perceive as innate in the present structure of your language, that you do not accept the 'steady state' theory of the universe. But such a position is, as I said, in error.

"The universe–or rather, that level of the universe which we all perceive–began some 12 billion years ago, it is true. But it will remain in existence far beyond the point at which we expect to meet the Worthy Ones."

"Ok, chew on that one, Robot," Will said, grinning. "I guess he told *you!*"

"I have the feeling we are talking around the point," Robinson said. "Can you explain more clearly just what is going on here–who you are, why you have done what you have done, and the rest of it?"

"It is a very long story indeed, Professor Robinson," said Gil'mish. "Perhaps if we seat ourselves, we will not tire in the telling."

And before anyone could mention that there were no seats to be seen, Gil'mish flicked a finger and seats appeared.

"I won't say anything. I won't. I won't," muttered Don under his breath, and sat down with the rest of them.

"I will not bore you with undue details," Gil'mish stated. "In essence it is a simple story–but I warn you that you may find aspects of it profoundly disturbing. My reading of your personality patterns assures me you can all of you sustain the information, but please understand.

"This is partly *your* story."

When the Home Galaxy of the Giandhu coalesced out of the inchoate random swirls of matter after the creation of the universe, the Gia sun was the first whose planets spawned life that survived to develop intelligence. That was almost ten billion years ago.

The Giandhu thus were the first race also to develop sufficient intelligence to construct star-traveling devices–though they were not space ships in the Earth sense of the terminology.

And for a billion years they were the only race to do so; for there were few races indeed at that dawn of time and space.

Because of this, the Giandhu steadily became masters of a greater and greater volume of space, until they spanned the entire galaxy and spread out to the next, and to the next after that, until, two and a half billion years after they began to conquer space, the Giandhu held five galaxies.

Alone in this gigantic multitude of stars and planets they held the key to space–intelligence.

Alone.

Like the present-day Ambarene they had their telepathic linkages; but time palled on them at last, and loneliness for something *beyond* the limits of their own intelligence began to tug destructively at the fabric of their lives.

And like the present-day Central Complex of the planet Voyd'azh, they made, at last, their attempts at directly forming another race of equal stature for themselves.

And failed.

Time after time they attempted to create directly another race of Worthy Ones, with whom they could live as equals, not as superiors.

And failed, time after time.

Intelligence, they could create; greatness, they could not.

At length a weariness, beyond their strength to resist, infected the Giandhu.

The Giandhu became weary unto death.

Some left for the trackless nameless galaxies beyond and were never heard from.

But many more simply allowed themselves to die.

Some elders debated pushing forward, deeper, all the race together, into the endless universe of galaxies to find a race of Worthy Ones.

Others counselled doing as a race what so many were doing individually–allowing themselves simply to die as they reached the end of their natural span by fore-going the treatments that kept them virtually immor-tal … without a purpose they could care about.

And a few counselled sleep–sleep in Giandahar, but with a purpose at last.

In the end, something over a million of them drew together at Giandahar–after seeding the Five Galaxies with life spores based on their own fundamental bio-chemical structure. But the spores were non-directed, so that what resulted would not simply be more Giandhu.

Then they made Giandahar a pleasure and delight for themselves, and a mystery and a puzzle, as they lived out their final era before sleep. And they directed the city to live on in peace after its long service to the race, maintaining itself only, and directing it simply to awaken one of them in turn, as races developed to the point where they could travel to the stars–and arrived thereafter at the Gia system.

Weaker races were not to trigger the awakening, however. These would be allowed to land, to test themselves involuntarily among the treasures and delectations of Giandahar; but if they failed, the city was to make them leave–gently, safely, and with no record and with no memory of what had been.

Many races, in spite of this, were advanced enough to trigger the city into awakening one of the sleepers, that he might judge more closely whether the visitors were truly Worthy Ones. Thirty thousand sleepers awakened one by one to judge such races, and thirty thousand times returned to sleep, the task again unsuccessful.

And again the failed ones left–gently, safely, and with no memory of the city or their actions.

But from that point on special monitors observed that race, and kept its ships in subtle ways from ever returning to the Gia system until such time as the race should grow in stature past the point where it was found wanting.

So far, no race had ever returned; while most went on to wreck themselves in futile wars and combats, losing forever their one chance for true immortality and power...

The ha-Grebst failed the city's basic tests; the Earthmen caused Gil'mish to wake.

And now the time of judgment was at hand...

"Judgment!" whispered Maureen.

"Immortality!" whispered Don, even lower, transfixed with the sudden brilliant dream.

"Boy," said Will in low tones, "I'll bet Dr. Smith will kick himself for not being here. All that talk about power–that's right up his alley!"

John Robinson looked at his hands abstractedly as he held them before his face; then he put them down again, and wondered why he'd done that.

"Do you realize," he started to say, and realized he had not spoken aloud.

"Do you realize," he said aloud, "the meaning of what Gil'mish has told us?"

The sound of his voice irritated him; it was shaking, as if he were afraid. He shut his eyes and made one brief futile attempt to convince himself he hadn't heard what Gil'mish had said.

The others were looking at him, rather startledly, more struck by the sound of his voice than by his words.

"He's...he's just told us...that the Giandhu was responsible for...for life on Earth. I mean..."

His voice broke in the confusion of his thought.

The full impact of it was too much for the others, he realized.

"Now wait," said Don. "Just a second. It's been estimated that life on Earth started about four billion years ago, right? And that back seven billion years ago, when the Giandhu went into hibernation, the Earth wasn't fit to support life. Therefore," he said, an incongruous note of pride in his voice, "that means life on Earth probably developed independently!"

Gil'mish stared at the rapidly-moving squiggles on the wall.

Then he spoke.

"The main banks have located your star as of the time of our … withdrawal. Nine planets. Second, third, fourth, and fifth from the sun were seeded. Hm, the fifth planet no longer exists as such.

"No, it is clear that you are directly descended from the original Giandhu spores."

Don worked his lips a couple of times, then gave up and accepted the concept.

"Whew!" Robinson said. "I guess that lays it on the line."

"No Adam and Eve?" Will asked Gil'mish, and the giant shook his head.

"No Adam and Eve, son," his father said, patting his shoulder with absent-minded affection while his eyes remained on the figure of Gil'mish. He felt vaguely disappointed that the others were not, apparently, anywhere nearly as deeply stirred by what had been said.

"But," he thought to himself, "it's really too much for me too. It's too much; I'll have to have more time to sort it out."

Aloud, he asked Gil'mish, "What I want to know is, what do we have to do now? Or rather, what do you intend to do?"

"First I must see your shipmates," Gil'mish answered with his slow deliberation. "My mind remains unduly sluggish; perhaps some slight dysfunction in the nutrient solution …"

"Well, I should think so, after all that time," said Maureen, with a surge of maternal instinct she was fully aware was quite misplaced.

"The seeds of a race's self-destruction are often buried deep within its members," Gil'mish said as he arose stiffly. "Let us proceed to the surface while I ponder."

And he vanished.

"Yipes!" said Will, and the rest of them caught their breaths.

"Well," said Don presently, and his tone was bitter, "I'll bet you one thing. If anything is wrong with humans, Gil'mish will find it in good old Dr. Zachary Smith. I'll tell you right now, though, if he does mess everything up I'll make him wish he–"

Robinson's face twisted with a wry smile.

"Don," he said softly, "try grading yourself on what you just said …"

Don looked at Professor Robinson blankly for a moment.

Then his face fell into a grimace of self-disgust. "Well, maybe it's just being around him that makes me think like that."

Will started to speak–and the room dissolved around them.

A moment later they were all standing on the familiar ground floor of the Central Tower, and Gil'mish was turning from one of the colored, animated wall-maps.

"My apologies," Gil'mish said slowly. "I forgot to bring you along."

He gestured at the wall-map; squiggles raced rapidly across it. "It seems we shall be in for a visit presently."

They looked blankly at the squiggles.

"Your Dr. Smith is leading the failed ones here," explained Gil'mish. "And your daughter is with him."

Don shook his head dubiously. "I don't think any good is going to come of this…"

"Aha!" said Smith, as he stood outside the Central Tower. "The immeasurable powers of this magnificent headset become more and more accessible to my mighty mind. My dear Judy, I can now sense with the aid of this marvelous gadget that the rest of the Jupiter II crew stands within these walls. Today the Jupiter II–tomorrow the galaxy!"

"Yes, master," said Judy tonelessly.

"Oh, stop that," Smith said testily. "Here…"

He squeezed his brows and concentrated on releasing Judy from the headset's control.

Judy staggered for a moment when his control ceased, then caught herself and drew up proudly.

"Dr. Smith," she said icily, "that was hardly the action of a gentleman. Or of a scholar, since it wasn't very smart of you."

"Child, you touch my pride," said Smith with warm indignation. "What better way to acquire an empress than to acquire one who will be in all things subservient to my wishes? Much the happiest way for any married man to enjoy his life…"

"You might just as well be married to the ship's robot," she retorted angrily. "And if I'm going to be an empress, at least I want to *know* about it. I felt like I was locked up tightly in a little room, bound and gagged."

"Ah!" Smith brightened. "Then you do still wish to become my empress! Wonderful! I shall–"

"You shall nothing. I meant you're not doing anybody any good by controlling them with that thing. It was like being in prison. Or worse. As for being your empress… well, that's out. You can always use your gadget, of course."

"Hmphh," Smith said. "If you feel that strongly about it, perhaps we'd better just forget the whole thing."

"Perhaps," she said, and looked away disinterestedly.

"Bah," Smith muttered, and scowled at the front of the Central Tower. "All right, open up, confound it. I haven't got all day. There's a universe out there waiting for me."

The wall dutifully opened up.

"Come along, then, my lovelies, step lively. You too, Judy. I don't want to lose track of you."

They followed him inside, the ha-Grebst docilely, Judy defiant.

Instinctively as the aliens entered the Robinsons and Don started to reach for their laser pistols, but Maureen rushed towards her daughter, meeting her halfway as they sobbed with relief in each other's arms.

"Ah, there," Smith began cheerfully, waving the weapons aside, "the Robinsons and Dr. West. How nice to see you once again and–awk! What's that?" He pointed at Gil'mish, who observed him calmly.

"That is Gil'mish," said Robinson. "It turns out that this is his city, not that of the ha-Grebst. We were hoping that he would help us rescue Judy from them, but you seem to have handled the matter adequately without us."

"Adequately! Oh, ho, ho, yes, oh, quite adequately indeed, I assure you!" Smith was highly elated. "Things are working out beautifully!"

"I'm glad you think so," Don said sourly. "I have a feeling you don't know what you're up against."

"Nonsense, my boy, I know exactly what I'm doing. First, I am going to send the ha-Grebst to their ship. Second, you will all proceed to the Jupiter II–along with this splendid-looking specimen. We will then fly in close formation to the home planet of the ha-Grebst, wherever it is, and I shall take it over. Time then to pause and consider the details of the next step."

"You *are* kidding," said Don. "I for one wouldn't so much as turn around for you."

Smith's smile was beautifully malicious. "Ah, but you most certainly would, dear boy..."

There was a slight pause.

Then Professor Don West, late of Cal Tech, threw his arms up in the air and began spinning around and around...

"Stop that," said Gil'mish.

"Pooh," said Smith. "You put your arms up and spin about too."

A weary smile creased Gil'mish's face. One arm went up, pointed at Smith–and the silvery headset vanished.

Smith screamed with horror as, his control over the ha-Grebst now gone, twelve rat-faced monstrosities shook themselves slowly and slowly looked at him and slowly advanced upon him...

"Oh, dear," said Judy, "they liked it even less than I did–poor Dr. Smith–save him!"

"Oh, yes, yes, yes, yes," shrieked Smith, falling to his knees and squeezing his eyes shut. "Save me! Save me! Oh, please, dear Mr. Gil'mish, don't let them get to me! Don't let them get me! Oh, woe, woe, mercy!" And he howled piteously.

Ignoring everyone else in the room, the ha-Grebst one by one shook off their stunned, dazed expressions and continued a relentless advance on the being who had dared to take their minds and bodies prisoner against their will–such an insult could only be wiped out in blood.

Rethog extended one clawlike hand for Smith's throat...

Gilmish waved his hand.

The twelve ha-Grebst vanished.

His eyes firmly shut, Smith continued to beg and howl for his life.

One by one, the Robinsons began to laugh in spite of themselves, with relief.

Smith opened his eyes. It took a moment for him to realize what had happened.

Then he moaned piteously, the last drop of arrogance temporarily squeezed out of him.

"Well, you don't have to tell us, Gil'mish," Don said with a sigh. "We don't make the grade either, right?"

Gil'mish nodded his head sadly. "Dr. Smith is what he is; weak, easily tempted. Here the temptation was too great, and hence he has in a way failed for all of you. But do not judge him too harshly among yourselves, for I tell you that the seeds of his actions are in all of you.

"Your race is strong and has much wisdom, and few races that have visited here have come closer. Humanity has a rare gift of genetic differentiation, so that your good and evil is distributed unevenly. The ha-Grebst, on the other hand, are, like the greatest number of races that have come here, more of a piece. Within another hundred years they will have destroyed themselves."

"We'll be lucky if *we* make it through the next hundred years," said Robinson. "Earth's history isn't one to delight the optimists."

"On the contrary," Gil'mish stated. "I perceive that many times you have had men of wisdom who led the way through dangers many other races would have succumbed to. Do not forget, also, that there is much good even in Dr. Smith. He is—"

Will could not contain himself. "He *is* good. He's kind and warm-hearted and he's my friend. He just ... he just gets carried away some times."

Gil'mish gestured at the boy. "There is much good in any man who can win the heart of a child. I do not mean to tell you that evil does not exist, or that you need not fight it, however.

"And do not forget one other thing. All men everywhere carry within them their own punishments and their own rewards—for each man can be and must be ... only what he is."

There was silence.

Will took a step forward, hesitated, then went to Dr. Smith and helped him to his feet, the Robot following as they walked slowly and silently to the building wall, which opened before them.

Gil'mish resumed.

"I see one last question that I can answer, in your mind, Penny. Yes, if the Ambroline came here, it would be quite possible that they would prove to be the Worthy Ones.

"But—the Ambroline have not come here. Nor do I think they ever will. They have found their way of life, the overmind, and it is theirs. We could perhaps by subtle means encourage them to develop space travel and make the journey here, and they might thank us for it—but such is not our way. We tried to influence other, long before, and in the long run it did not ever work.

"Your instruments are repaired, your fuel tanks are full. Sufficient stocks of food, water, and oxygen are now aboard the Jupiter II.

"I shall return to sleep once more, and you must leave before I do. I grant you our last age-old gift, of forgetfulness, once you are safely off the planet and have set your course.

"Farewell…"

Gil'mish and the room faded from their eyes, to be replaced by the interior of the Jupiter II.

"Sheesh!" Don said, "I wish he didn't zip us around so fast. Hope he's going to let us lift off under our own steam!"

Robinson checked the instruments. "I think he is– but as a gentle hint, the thrusters are warm and ready for firing. It looks like there's a course programmed into the main computer banks, too."

"Yeah?" Don sat in his accustomed seat and punched the read-out button. Figures and words sped rapidly by on the fluorescent screen.

"How about that!" he said. "I hope everybody's strapped in. If so, we can take off in…" He studied the screen. "Mark three minutes"

"Ai-yi!" Robinson said, and slapped his forehead. "We didn't even ask him if he'd send us home to Earth!"

A pseudo-voice filled the control room of the Jupiter.

"I would not have, even had you asked. But I kept you from thinking of it till now, so that the thought would be least painful to you since you will soon forget. Your ship is lost; I am sorry, but it must continue as it has in the past. If you are to reach home it must be from your own efforts. This is necessary for us–and it is necessary for you, though you do not understand why."

The resonant pseudo-voice ceased.

Don and Robinson looked at each other; both sighed.

"I guess it won't make much difference," Robinson said. "We're going to forget all this anyway."

"Right," sighed Don. "Ok, let's check out the readings. Mark two minutes till lift-off."

The two went through the complex checkout procedures without a hitch.

"Mark one for lift-off," Don said.

"Okay," said Robinson, and picked up his communicator.

"Everyone strapped in?" he asked. "Will, how is Dr. Smith? He looked a little rocky when you helped him away."

"Oh, he'll be okay," Will's voice answered. "He's just a little depressed."

"Depressed, is it," Smith's voice came, "why, you foolish boy, I had a galaxy in the palm of my hands. Of course I'm depressed. I had such plans, such plans … and you say I'm depressed. My boy, I shall never recover from my present downcast state of mind. Oh, the pain, the pain! All that was worthwhile in life to me is now merely ashes, bitter ashes, in my mouth, which reminds me, Mrs. Robinson. We haven't eaten all day. Can I hope that we may have one of your excellent suppers as soon as we reach a stable course?"

Don grinned. *"He's* back to normal. Let's get out of here!"

Professor John Robinson, de facto captain of the Jupiter II, reached out to the pressure panel that would fire the main thrustors–and paused just before touching the panel.

"I don't *want* to leave!" he thought desperately to himself. "We had so much, so very much, within our grasp! There's still so much there we could use, things that could benefit humanity–incalculable treasures! I don't want to forget–I want to remember!"

"You must press the button," a gentle voice said in his mind.

"Yes," his own mind answered involuntarily.

And, convulsively, he stabbed the pressure panel with his forefinger.

In the three seconds before the thrustors built up power, he thought, trying to aim his thoughts at Gil'mish, "I understand. We must not be given these things. It would destroy our race. We must earn what we gain–strive for it, losing some times, winning some others.

"Nobody's ever given the human race anything so far, and it's still around.

"I guess it can pretty well manage to work out its own future."

"Yes," came the quiet thought, for the last time.

The thrustors caught, and the ship moved upwards, slowly, then faster and faster, as the ship rose majestically off the impervious blue translucent surface of the

Central Plaza of the city of Giandahar, ten billion years old, and as the ship plunged upward through the rapidly thinning atmosphere, all memories of Giandahar faded away–all sadness, and all happiness.

And all regrets.

Lost among the infinite patchwork blacknesses between the endless stars, the lonely ship moved onwards through the trackless wildernesses of the infinite universe.